"You need another partner."

"You're going to need a consultant before the summer is through. I've just dropped by to offer my services," Victoria said.

"I thought you were going to camp." To my relief, Lizzie had finally spoken up.

"Not until the last week in August," Victoria informed her. "I'll be available to consult until then."

"We don't need a consultant," Buck said. "The four of us are equal partners. We can handle things just fine. We vote on everything anyway."

"What happens if it's two against two?" Victoria asked. "What you need is another partner. Someone who knows the inside track of business. Someone like me."

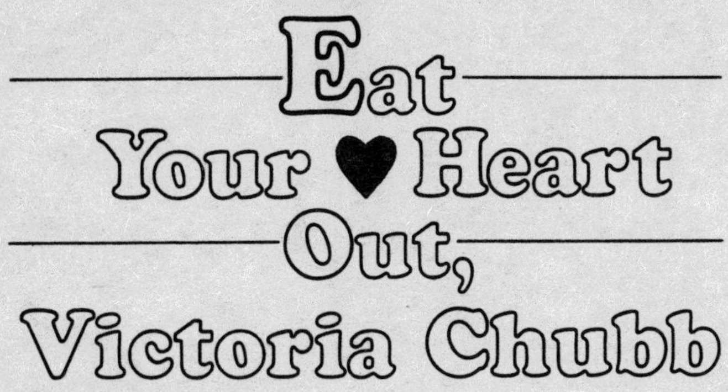

Joyce Hunt

SCHOLASTIC INC.
New York Toronto London Auckland Sydney

ISBN 0-590-42554-4

12 11 10 9 8 7 6 5 4 3 2 1 2 3 4 5/9

Printed in the U.S.A. 28

First Scholastic printing, January 1990

This book is dedicated with special thanks to the members of our Albany Writers' Group, who have listened and encouraged for years.

1

Aces, The Kids' Luncheonette and Delivery Service, might never have started if the four of us hadn't been sitting on my front steps that first Monday morning of summer vacation. We were already feeling so bored that we were starting to pick on each other. The four of us are Gina Lazzaro, Lizzie (Elizabeth) Tanner, Edward Buckley (known to everyone except his parents as Buck), and me, Roger Gordon.

The four of us have known each other for five of our twelve years. We were all part of a neighborhood group my father calls The Pioneers. By that he means that our four families were among the first twenty families who bought homes in Forest Estates years ago, when this area was a brand-new development. To hear my father talk you'd think we were just like real pioneers living in a wagon train. "There were no sidewalks, no streetlights, and no grass that first year," he's told me several times. Now, with over two hundred homes in the development, in every size, shape, and color, it's hard to believe that our community was once a huge, grassy meadow.

I met Buck when I was four. He lives around the corner, and one day when my mother had taken me for a walk we ran into him and his mom. Mrs. Buckley, who is short and a little plump like Buck, invited my mother in to sample a piece of warm coffee cake, while Buck invited me to try his squeaky new swing set. "My mother calls me Edward, but my real name is Buck," he told me as we tried to see who could swing the highest.

"This is a neat swing set, Buck," I said.

He and I have been best friends ever since.

We got to know Lizzie and Gina the following year at the bus stop, waiting to go to kindergarten. Mrs. Lazzaro was trying to get Gina to stop crying before the bus came, and suddenly Buck and I, who felt like crying ourselves, started to kid around, trying to make Gina laugh. Lizzie began to giggle, pretty soon Gina was smiling, too, and by the time the bus arrived we couldn't wait to get to school. Luckily we all ended up in Miss Fisher's kindergarten. Back then we'd meet after school to play in someone's yard, and we've been hanging around together ever since.

On that particular summer morning Gina and

Lizzie were curled up in my parents' plastic lawn chairs. "My new baby brother woke me up at one, three, five, and seven," Gina had told us. "Don't wake me up if I fall asleep in this chair."

Buck and I were slouched on the steps at their feet. We'd stopped talking about how glad we were that the final days of school were over at last. Now we were tiring ourselves out by doing nothing. Actually, we were worse than bored. Each of us, for a different reason, was feeling angry and gypped that summer.

My reason for feeling angry and gypped was that my mother had gone back to work in the spring. It started out innocently enough, with a real estate course at the community college. The next thing we knew, she had sold one house, listed two more, and declared she'd never known you could have such a good time working. How anyone could have a good time working I couldn't understand.

Also that summer, my seventeen-year-old brother, Tommy, was working for money to pay for college. Tommy did not pretend he was having a good time. He spent his nights delivering pizza for The Italian Connection, which meant that he slept all day. Unless it was a desperate emergency, my brother made it clear he was not to be awakened. He slept with his earphones on and his head buried under his pillows from seven in the morning until three in the afternoon. Then he went to the mall. The house was so quiet all day I couldn't stand it!

"There're always plenty of little tasks you could do around the house, Roger," my mother was fond of telling me. That was another drawback to her job. Those days a lot of the housework had to be done by my dad, Tommy, and worst of all, me. It wasn't something we were eager to get used to doing.

"Quit feeding the ants," I grumbled at Buck that Monday morning. He was shaking stale cracker crumbs out of the corner of his jeans pockets and dropping them in front of the big black ants that were crawling through the grass along the steps. As he leaned forward his glasses slid toward the tip of his nose, and a strand of brown hair fell, almost covering his eyes. In kindergarten Miss Fisher used to tease Buck by asking him if he was allergic to haircuts. Now, even though he'd finished sixth grade, it looked as if he still had that allergy.

"Just because you like to eat twenty-four hours a day doesn't mean you have to throw food at everything that moves," I told him.

Buck glared at me, then rolled his eyes and said haughtily, "I don't eat when I'm sleeping, Roger.

So I couldn't possibly eat twenty-four hours a day."

"Then make it sixteen. Just quit feeding the ants," I snapped. Even though Buck was my best friend, at times he could get on my nerves. I suppose I got on his nerves, too, and though he'd never said it, I sometimes got the feeling he was a little envious of the way I'd shot up in the last year. I was almost as tall as my dad, and about a head taller than Buck, who still had some of his baby fat as well.

"I suppose you own these ants, Roger?" Buck asked, pushing the glasses back up on his nose and his hair out of his face.

"This is my yard," I said. "I control what goes on here."

I was purposely being mean to Buck, whom I knew was sensitive these days, especially on the subject of food. Since May his mother had had the entire family on a no-sweets diet. Buck was grouchy from ice-cream-and-cake deprivation.

"Cut it out, you two," Lizzie said. She was leafing through an old *Spiderman* comic, which for Lizzie Tanner, the smartest kid in the sixth grade, meant things were pretty bad. "When's the weather supposed to warm up?" she asked with a shiver that shook her shoulders and made her long brown hair, pulled into a ponytail today, quiver. "Usually in July the average temperature is seventy-four degrees." This is the sort of fact Lizzie will throw into conversation when you are least expecting it, not to sound smart, but just because it's something she happens to know. Lizzie is almost as tall as I am, with clear blue eyes and a nice smile you don't see as much anymore since she got braces on her teeth.

"It's not supposed to warm up until early next week," Gina said. "My toes are freezing, but I refuse to wear anything but sandals. I didn't paint my toenails purple for nothing."

Gina hadn't been the same since her colicky baby brother, Lester Winchell Lazzaro II, had been born two months before. She insisted that no one in her house has slept through the night since then, and even the waking hours haven't been that pleasant. For some reason Gina turned to clothes and makeup to make this situation more bearable. Except for complaining about Lester, fashion is all she thought about those days.

In addition to our various troubles at home, the weather had played a rotten trick on us and clobbered us with a cold spell. Instead of turning up warm and sunny, the first days of our vacation had been damp, chilly, and dark. Forget the local pool where we'd planned to hang out all summer; forget begging some of the older kids to take us to a lake. We were stuck in the middle of suburbia.

"Victoria Chubb is going off to camp," Lizzie announced, not even lifting her blue eyes from *Spiderman.* Lizzie has this thing for people who go "off to camp" because her dad, who's a pretty well-known attorney, was presently "off to camp" himself. Every summer he goes to golf camp, a fact that Lizzie and her mother find hard to face. Even though the whole family takes a trip somewhere over winter break, Lizzie and Mrs. Tanner insist they need a summer vacation, too. But every summer Mr. Tanner golfs.

"I hate camp," Buck stated. "And I would hate any camp that had Victoria Chubb at it even more."

Gina and I both nodded in agreement. Victoria Chubb is the biggest snob at Lincoln Middle School. I was glad that she was being sent to camp.

"Not regular camp," Lizzie explained. "She's going to an investment camp, where they teach you how to invest wisely in the stock market so you make a lot of money. I heard Victoria telling some kids at school that her parents think it's time she started to learn about the family business. They're giving her five hundred dollars to play with. She says she's going to double it."

"Five hundred dollars!" Gina gasped, suddenly

wide awake. "Do you have any idea the clothes I could buy with five hundred dollars? And I'd have my hair done at Jacques', too. He charges fifty dollars for a cut. But it's worth it. I wish I were Victoria Chubb."

Victoria Chubb lives at the farthest end of our development in a section that has new, huge, modern houses. My father says he couldn't even afford to buy the garages on most of those homes, but then he always adds that he's perfectly happy with what we have. So am I. I'm just not happy when I hear about Victoria Chubb, who happens to be one of the biggest know-it-alls I've ever met.

"Whoopie hoot for Victoria Chubb!" I cried. "I'll bet I can double my money faster than she can."

"All you'd have to do is find another penny on the sidewalk and your money would be doubled," Buck said. Lizzie and Gina giggled.

"Very funny," I said. "It just so happens I have thirty dollars stashed away. And given the right opportunity, I bet I could turn it into sixty. Possibly even a hundred and twenty. And I wouldn't have to go to investment camp to do it, either."

Actually I'm a pretty quiet person. Usually I don't shoot off my mouth or brag. But I was feeling irritable because the summer, which I'd always loved, just wasn't the same that year.

"So how would you do it, Roger?" Lizzie challenged.

I shrugged. "I don't know," I said.

I looked up and down Fern Street. There were about a dozen little kids in shorts, shirts, and sneakers scattered in clusters, playing on bikes and with balls and wagons. On every street in our area, on Pine, Oak, Apple, and Lilac, it was the same.

From what I've learned from my mother's real estate conversations, most of the houses around here are either what she calls two-story colonials or split-level ranches. They are three- or four-bedroom homes with big yards and lots of trees, great for families. That is why people move here, so their kids will have lots of other kids to play with.

"I'd start a business," I said. "A business for little kids."

"What kind of business?" Buck asked. "You never know; if it's good enough, I just might want to invest part of my immense fortune in it, too."

Even though I knew that Buck was only kidding around, his idea appealed to me. I liked the way I felt when I thought about starting a business; I liked the grown-up way I sounded when I talked about it. And just suppose I did start a business?

Suppose I did show that creepy Victoria Chubb, and everyone who was working, that I could make money just as well as they could?

"First," I said, "I'd have to figure out what kids like."

"Toys," Buck said. "I can't wait to see the world's first thirty-dollar toy store."

"I wouldn't open a toy store," I retorted.

"Kids love TV," Buck said. "For thirty dollars maybe you can start your own TV channel."

"Very funny," I said, blowing a cracker crumb out of the feelers of a determined ant who was trying to drag it away.

"Food!" Lizzie exclaimed. "Kids like food."

"So why don't you open a restaurant?" Buck said, poking me in the arm. "A restaurant for all the little kids in this neighborhood. You could feature the best peanut-butter-and-jelly sandwiches on the east coast."

Even though we knew he was still kidding around, Gina, Lizzie, and I looked at each other. I shrugged, trying to seem casual. But inside I was starting to feel the first prickles of excitement I'd felt since school officially got out. I could almost picture my restaurant. It would be a smaller version of the school cafeteria. But instead of "bland, canned, and poorly planned," which was how we described the school food, my restaurant would aim to *please* kids' tastes.

"Of course, I'd have to start out small," I began. Half closing my eyes, I looked into the distance, across the street, and beyond all the rows of houses that were not terribly different from my own. The vision became clearer.

Buck leaned forward, suddenly very interested. "Like how small?" he asked.

"I would probably serve only lunch at first," I said slowly. "Most kids like to have breakfast and dinner at home. I would call the restaurant The Kids' Luncheonette," I decided. "And each three-course meal would cost only one dollar."

"Where would this luncheonette be?" Buck asked.

Again I surveyed Fern Street. Small kids were zooming by on tricycles, scooters, and skates. They were doing the same thing on every block for miles around, while inside their houses parents and baby-sitters were wondering what to serve them for lunch. I turned and pointed to my own garage, where my parents' two cars were usually parked. In the corner was our old refrigerator, called into service when there was a big sale on frozen foods, but otherwise empty. Above it all my brother slept blissfully, his blaring headphones blocking out any bothersome noises.

"How about right here?" I asked, pointing to the space between the gas grill and two shiny bikes.

Gina's eyes were glittering as if little sparklers had been lit behind them. "Can I apply for a job right now?" she asked.

Even Buck was being drawn in. "How much money do you think we'd need?"

Lizzie, whom I'd always admired for her great intelligence, only smiled. "Brilliant, Roger," she said, dropping the *Spiderman* comic at last. "I think we've come up with a simply brilliant idea."

2

The first business meeting of The Kids' Luncheonette was held in my bedroom at noon that very same Monday. I sat on the edge of the bed with a notebook, ready to take notes. Buck, who had plopped himself in my beanbag chair, had brought a bag of coconut-marshmallow puffs and a two-liter bottle of Coke, because he claimed executives always had food at their noontime meetings. Lizzie was leaning against a pillow at the head of the bed, holding a piece of paper covered with notes, the result of an hour's worth of research she'd done on our neighborhood. Gina, who had brought a calculator and a book with her, took the position of authority and sat at my desk.

" 'Decide upon the need you'll serve,' " she read aloud from the book, which she'd taken out of the library. The book was called *Now You're the Boss*, and the librarian had told her it was just what she was looking for. "This will show you step-by-step how to start your own little enterprise," the librarian had said, giving Gina the distinct impression that the librarian hoped our corner 10-cent lemonade stand would be a raving success.

"The need is food," Buck said, stuffing a whole marshmallow puff into his mouth. His pudgy cheeks grew fuller as he chewed it.

"I think we have to be a little more specific," Lizzie said. Because her father is a lawyer, and because she wants to be a lawyer when she gets older, Lizzie can be very serious about words. "The need is *lunch.* Lunch for the little kids in this neighborhood. According to my findings, there are over one hundred kids living within five blocks of this house."

"Which five blocks?" Buck asked, unscrewing the Coke-bottle cap.

"Just one minute, Buck!" Gina interrupted, pushing back my desk chair. "If we're going to share that Coke, you can't drink it right out of the bottle. I will not put my lips where yours have been."

"Who says we're gonna share it?" Buck asked. "And who says I would even let your sticky smackers anywhere near my Coke bottle?" I knew Buck was referring to the grape-flavored lip gloss Gina was forever smearing on her lips, and I didn't think his remark was fitting at an executive meeting.

"Look, you guys," I said, standing up. "This is a serious business meeting."

"This is a serious bottle of Coke," Buck retorted. Gina laughed, and even Lizzie smiled, showing a glimmer of silver braces.

"Oh, boy," I said, "hold on."

I ran to the bathroom and pulled four little flowered paper cups out of the dispenser. My mom tells us to use them when someone in the family is sick and she doesn't want germs spread by the yellow plastic cup. I tiptoed past the tightly closed door that isolated my sleeping brother from all daytime noises. "Here," I said, tossing a paper cup to each of my friends. "And keep it down. Tommy's sleeping. Now are we ready to proceed?"

"Yep," Buck said as he carefully poured four tiny servings of Coke. "I believe I was asking Lizzie which five blocks she was talking about, before I was so ungraciously interrupted."

Gina made a face at him, but she let Lizzie answer. "Five blocks in all four directions," Lizzie explained. "Five square blocks." Even leaning against pillows Lizzie could still seem like an authority.

"I see," Buck said, adjusting his glasses thoughtfully.

"So if we make one hundred lunches for a dollar a lunch we'd make a hundred dollars." Quickly Gina punched a few numbers on her calculator. "Or a hundred-and-twenty-five dollars if we charge a dollar-twenty-five. Eat your heart out, Victoria Chubb."

"We can't expect to sell one hundred lunches a day," I said. "Not all the kids will be around every day. Not all the mothers will want to buy them lunch here, either. Besides, Gina, lunches don't just appear. We're going to have to make them. Which means buying ingredients."

"I was going to figure in expenses," Gina said, opening her book again.

"We have to come up with a menu to start with," Lizzie interrupted.

" 'Keep it simple,' " Gina read, skipping a few pages ahead in *Now You're the Boss*. With fingernails painted a shiny purplish-red, she pointed to the page. "In other words, don't bite off more than you can chew. Get it?"

Ignoring Gina's humor, Lizzie proceeded in a very businesslike manner. "We need to come up with a simple menu. Maybe three kinds of sandwiches, two drinks, and three desserts. How does that sound?"

"All for a dollar? It sounds super," Buck said. "I'll take one of each. And make that to go."

Gina said, "Roger, please get a ruler. Draw three columns on that page. We can list choices, and the kids can pick one from each column. Like you do in a Chinese restaurant. Then they can come through the line and tell us what they want, and we can put all their selections in paper bags, collect a dollar from each of them, and send them off to eat them."

We all stared appreciatively at Gina as I rifled through my desk drawer to find a ruler. The picture she painted was very simple and clear. Along with purple lips and toenails, Gina also had a pretty good brain.

Lizzie nodded enthusiastically. "I can see it working," she said. "I can see them lined up right in this driveway for lunch."

"We'll have to advertise," Buck added. "Can I be in charge of promotion?"

"Sure," I said, carefully drawing two straight lines down the page. I felt excited. "Buck is my choice for Head of Promotion," I said. "Does anyone disagree?"

Gina and Lizzie shook their heads. Buck beamed. "Watch out, McDonald's!" he warned.

"I will be Head of Budget," Gina announced, digging her purple gloss out of her jeans pocket and running it along her lips. "But raising the initial capital is a crucial point according to this book. 'Do not risk everything,' it says."

For a second no one spoke. Then I said grandly, "I'm willing to put up twenty dollars to start out."

Buck frowned, then said, "I could come up with twenty dollars I guess. Of course, I'll need some of it back to pay for the ad campaign."

"I've got twenty dollars at home," Lizzie said. "I was going to use it to buy my own copy of *The Guinness Book of World Records*. But I suppose I could use the library copy for a while longer."

"I'll have to take it out of my savings account," Gina admitted. "But when I tell my mother how I'm going to double it, I'm sure she won't mind."

With that, Lizzie and I exchanged concerned looks. I knew we were both thinking the same thing. It wasn't that we wanted to be sneaky. We just wanted to wait before going public to our parents with an idea that they might not like.

"Uh, Gina," I said, "do you think you could get ahold of the money without telling your mother? Not that you can't tell her eventually," I added quickly. "But why not wait until the luncheonette is in full swing before you break the news that you're one of the partners?"

"Roger's right," Lizzie agreed. "No point in looking for trouble before we even begin. Not that your mother would cause trouble, Gina," she added. "You know what I mean."

"I guess I could," Gina said hesitantly. "I mean, it is *my* savings account. I was going to use the money to buy this tweed jacket with real fur trim I saw a couple of weeks ago. I was waiting until it went on sale. But I suppose I can just go to the bank and take out twenty dollars. No one even has to know."

"Only your teller knows for sure," Buck said with a wink.

"Do you know how many poor animals had to die to put real fur trim on that coat?" Lizzie asked.

"So the financing is settled," I said quickly. There wasn't time now for a debate on animal rights. "We have eighty dollars for food and advertising," I summarized aloud as I wrote a new page. "Gina is Head of Budget. Buck is Head of Promotion." I paused and looked up. Even though my brother Tommy is six years older than me, he sometimes says I'm too bossy. I wanted to be sure no one here was thinking that. But they didn't seem to be, so I went on.

"Today is Monday. If we can come up with a menu, buy food, and have posters ready to put up by tomorrow, I bet we could open on Wednesday."

"The Grand Opening," Buck said dreamily. "I'll need money for balloons, streamers, signs. . . ."

"Hold on, Buck," Gina said firmly.

"Our menu has to come first," Lizzie reminded him. "You're going to have to develop a better business sense. The product is the first thing to worry about."

"It's when no one *knows* about the product that you have to worry," Buck countered. "Advertising is the key to every successful business venture."

"The first column will list the sandwich choices," Gina said, ignoring their bickering and pointing to the neatly divided sheet where I had drawn the columns. "Peanut butter and jelly will be first," she said. "On your choice of wheat or white." I nodded and wrote it down.

"How about peanut butter and marshmallow fluff?" I asked. "Kids love that."

"But most mothers would think it's too sticky and sweet," Lizzie pointed out, being realistic. "They'll worry about cavities."

"So? Isn't this a restaurant for kids?" I asked.

"The parents are paying," Lizzie reminded me.

"She's right," Gina said. "How about tuna and bologna instead?"

We all agreed on that, and I wrote it down. "Drinks?" I questioned.

"We'll have to have milk," Lizzie declared. "And some kind of juice. Maybe we could get those variety packs of fruit juices." Everyone nodded, and I scribbled furiously. Suddenly the menu was shaping up before our eyes. "Dessert?" I asked.

"Fruit," Lizzie said.

"Brownies, cookies, and cake," Buck suggested. "All homemade, of course."

"And who's going to make them?" I asked.

"Well, I sure can't," Buck said defensively. "My mother would go berserk if I started baking brownies while she's got us all on that diet." But a far-away look came into his eyes and I was sure he was imagining himself in front of a plate full of rich, chocolaty treats that his mother knew nothing about.

Gina shook her head, too. "I don't dare enter the kitchen these days, with all the formula and bottles around."

"I will be in charge of desserts," Lizzie said, words as sweet to my ears as the cookies, cakes, and brownies themselves.

"I could help you," Buck offered. "If we did the baking at your house it would be no problem. My mother couldn't object then." And you can sample from each batch, I thought.

"OK," Lizzie said. "Make that, Buck and I are in charge of desserts," she told me.

"Then let's go!" I said loudly. "Everyone head home — or wherever you have to go to get your money. It's one-thirty now. We'll meet back here at three. And bring along anything you have that we might be able to use. Everybody set?"

"Yes," Gina said.

"Yep," Buck added.

"Set," Lizzie confirmed.

And with that, the first meeting of The Kids' Luncheonette broke up.

3

At three o'clock Gina tossed a crisp twenty-dollar bill on my desk, then pulled out the chair, sat down, and glossed her lips. Lizzie brought in two tens. Buck had a five, a ten, three ones, and two handfuls of change, and I had four fives. Eighty dollars, no matter how you counted it, was piled before us on my desk.

"Some large corporations spend almost half their money on advertising," Buck told us. He was munching from a bag of popcorn, which he passed around to everyone except Lizzie, who said no thanks because of her braces.

"Well this one isn't going to," I said.

"What makes *you* the authority?" Buck asked me.

"*My* garage, *my* bedroom, *my* idea to start with," I chanted at Buck.

"*My* markers, *my* poster board, *my* hammer, *my* nails," Buck chanted back.

"You two are about as grown-up as *my* baby brother," Gina said with disgust. "We're all putting in the same amount of money, so we're all equal partners. Besides, we'll never get anywhere if we keep fighting with each other."

"Gina's right," Lizzie said. "We'll have to vote on everything, Roger. Just because the luncheonette is in your garage, and we're at your house, doesn't mean you're running things."

"Yeah," Buck said, making a face at me.

"Cut it out, Buck," Lizzie warned. "It was everyone's idea, and I don't want to see it ruined by you two fighting over stupid things." Her voice had that I-mean-business sound I thought only teachers and parents could make. That was a funny thing about Lizzie. She wore regular jeans and sweatshirts, she didn't fuss with her long brown hair or wear makeup, and she still looked like a little kid. But she could seem a lot more grown-up than the rest of us lots of the time.

"Fine with me," I said. I did agree with her. Who cared, really, whose idea it was? The point was to get it going.

"OK," Lizzie said. "Then let's vote on our advertising budget. What kind of advertising are you going to do, Buck?"

"Signs," Buck said. "Lots of signs. On trees,

telephone poles, mailboxes. You know, all over."

"It's against the law to put anything on a mailbox," Lizzie informed him. "So you've got the markers and that pile of poster board. How much more do you need?"

"Ten dollars," Buck said.

I frowned and shook my head, but I didn't say a word. Gina looked puzzled. "Ten dollars for what?" she asked.

"These markers are old and dry," Buck said. "They're not going to last long."

"And they cost $2.29," Gina told him, pointing to the orange price sticker.

"Plus tax," Buck argued, shaking the last crumbs of popcorn into his hand.

"I think your budget should be three dollars to start with," Lizzie decided. Buck began to object. "OK, we'll vote on it," Lizzie said. "Raise your hand if you think three dollars is a good advertising budget for Buck. To start with," she stressed, trying to soften the blow.

Gina, Lizzie, and I raised our hands. Mine went the highest. Buck shook his head. "Don't blame me if this whole thing flops," he grumbled. "Three dollars for advertising!" We all ignored him.

"The food budget is next," I said. "How many vote for seventy-seven dollars for the food budget?" That was the amount of money left over when Buck's advertising budget was subtracted from the total. I raised my hand. Gina started to raise hers, too.

"I object!" Buck cried. "I think we should keep some money aside in case of emergency. Suppose there's a crisis in advertising? There won't be any money left over."

"What do you think, Lizzie?" I asked. I had always known Lizzie was smart. But I was starting to learn she was sensible and fair, too.

"We should probably put ten dollars aside just in case," Lizzie said. "Which would give us sixty-seven dollars for food."

"Is that enough money?" Gina asked. "If food prices are anything like clothes prices we may not have enough. We'd better make a list and see what we need, first."

Before we could start the list, however, there was a sharp knock at my door. "Hey, Roger? What are you doing?" Tommy's voice, still heavy with sleep, startled us all. I dove for the money, scooped up the cash, stuffed it in the top desk drawer, and then answered innocently, "Just hanging around with some of the guys from school. Come on in."

My brother poked his head in. His eyes were

still a little puffy, and the carefully unshaven line above his lips looked darker. For college, Tommy had decided to grow a mustache. He was worried that he looked too young. Now his hair was still damp from his shower, and he was smoothing down a slightly wrinkled T-shirt as he talked to us. "I'm heading to the mall, then I'm going to work. Tell Mom I'm meeting Cindy for dinner on her break, so I won't be eating here."

Cindy is Tommy's new girlfriend. My mother hasn't come right out and said it, but I get the feeling she's not too fond of Cindy. During the school year Cindy had called my brother at least four times a day.

"I'll tell her, but she's not going to like it," I said.

"Let me worry about that," my brother retorted. He looked at the four of us, who were gazing solemnly at him. "Why don't you guys find something interesting to do? You don't know how lucky you are not to have to work all summer."

Gina giggled.

"We're lucky, all right," Buck said. "We're probably the luckiest people in the entire world." We all started to laugh.

Tommy gave us a strange look. "I'll see you later," he said.

The door closed behind him, and Gina let out another giggle. "Your brother is so cute," she said, pulling a comb from her pocket and running it through her short bangs.

"That's not the word I'd use," I told her, even though I was sort of flattered. Lots of people thought I looked just like Tommy. We both had sandy brown hair, blue eyes, and long legs like my dad. "Tommy may have been cute the first few years of his life," I said. "But he's not cute anymore."

"Yes, he is," Gina said. "Right, Lizzie?"

"It's all a matter of opinion," Lizzie said. "Now, where were we? Oh, yes, the list. We need peanut butter, jelly, bologna, tuna fish, mustard, mayonnaise, bread. What else?"

"Milk and juice," Gina added. "And I still say he's cute."

"I think we should count on having sixty kids," Lizzie said. "We'll make twenty of each kind of sandwich. We'll need plastic sandwich bags and brown paper bags. I guess he *is* cute. I like the mustache."

I decided then and there to see if I could grow a mustache when I got older. Even though I would never admit it to anyone, Lizzie's opinion meant a lot to me.

"Put straws on that list," Buck said. "Maybe I'll grow a mustache over the summer," he said, reading my mind. "And what about dessert?"

We all turned to Lizzie. Dessert was the one thing that bothered me. I knew how little kids could be; dessert could make or break us.

"Put apples on the list to satisfy the parents," Lizzie directed. "And I was thinking of making M&M cookies. You know, the real big ones. They're delicious and colorful. Besides, we need a gimmick, and little kids love M&M's."

Everyone agreed, especially Buck. "You're a genius, Lizzie," he said. "A business wizard. And if you need any help making the cookies, when my advertising work is over I'll be glad to assist you, like I said before."

"I *will* need someone to help," Lizzie said. "I can make the mix. But I'll need someone to carefully take one batch off the sheets while I put another batch in to bake."

"I could do that," Buck volunteered. It wasn't hard for me to imagine how Buck would help make the cookies. He'd help *himself* to as many as he could eat!

"My mom won't be home tomorrow," Lizzie added. "She's going to visit my grandmother. And my dad's still at golf camp. So all I need to buy for the cookies is M&M's. Everything else I can use from home. Can you come over around six tomorrow, Buck?"

"Sure," Buck told her. "And I'll be glad to test each batch to make sure the quality is the same every time," he offered. Lizzie looked at him with a combination of amusement and impatience. But she didn't say a thing.

"So," I said, consulting the list. "It looks like we've got everything under control. Now, should we shop or advertise first?"

"Advertise," Gina and Buck said.

"Shop," Lizzie and I said in unison.

"Vote," I said.

"I'm voting with Buck on this one," Gina explained. "I think we should buy the food tomorrow. That way it will be fresher when we open."

"That's a good idea," Lizzie agreed.

I nodded and added my vote.

"Then let me show you what I have in mind for the posters," Buck said happily.

Actually, I had forgotten how artistic Buck could be. The posters he designed were pretty neat. They had brightly colored round balloons lining all four sides, and in big, black letters he'd written:

GRAND OPENING!
WEDNESDAY
THE FIRST — THE ONLY
KIDS' LUNCHEONETTE
FROM 11:30 to 1:00
EVERY LUNCH JUST ONE DOLLAR!
AT 12 FERN STREET
ALL KIDS WELCOME!!!

"It's great!" Gina said.

Buck beamed.

"Perfect," Lizzie added. "And it's so simple we can all copy it easily."

Which is what we did for the rest of the afternoon. By five o'clock there was a neat pile of posters announcing the Grand Opening of The Kid's Luncheonette stacked in the corner of my room. I tended to copy Buck's poster each time. But Gina, Lizzie, and Buck made new ones with flowers, hearts, and clowns scattered over them. I turned the front of the posters to the wall. Now that my mother was working she didn't come in to inspect my room very often like she used to. Still, I wasn't about to take any chances with someone seeing them. There would be plenty of time to tell my parents about this business idea when it was a big success.

"Meet back here tomorrow morning at nine," I instructed everyone as they left. "Tomorrow's a big day. We've got to do the shopping, put up the posters, and get the sandwiches and cookies made."

"Nothing to it," Buck declared.

"I've got to look for that recipe," Lizzie murmured.

"This is the most fun I've ever had on a summer vacation," Gina called.

And as I shut the door behind her I decided I couldn't agree with her more.

4

So, Roger," my mother said at dinnertime that evening as she arranged french fries on a plate to go into the microwave. "How did your first official day of summer vacation go?"

"OK," I said. "The weather was rotten, so I had some of the kids from school come over."

"Who'd you have in?" she asked. My mom loves to hear the details of my day even if it's just the same old school routine. She also loves to tell me the details of her days, the new houses she's seen, the people she's met, and the wild ways some people have of decorating and keeping their homes.

"Buck, Lizzie, and Gina came over," I said.

"How's Lizzie's dad?" my mom asked. "Is he home yet?" Everyone in town knows Mr. Tanner is a golf nut. And a lot of people, who feel the same way he does about golf, envy him his summer camp days. My mom is one of those people.

"Not yet. Lizzie and her mother wanted to go to the Cape this summer," I told her. "But they're going to go in the fall instead. Lizzie gets to miss three days of school then, so she's a little happier about it."

"How's Gina?"

"She's OK," I said.

"I saw her mother at the supermarket with the new baby. He never stopped crying — not for one minute — the whole time that poor woman shopped. Up one aisle and down the next, you could hear the baby wailing all over the store."

"Gina says he's got colic," I said.

"He sure does," my mother said with a smile. "Remember a few years ago when you wanted a baby brother?"

"Not really," I said. My mother loves to remind me of the jerky things I said and did as a kid. That and going through photo albums of Tommy and me when we still believed in Santa Claus are among her favorite pastimes. "Can I light the grill, Dad?"

My father had come into the kitchen with his fire wand, the long, pencil-shaped lighter he uses to ignite the gas grill. "Sure," he said, handing me the wand. "Where's Tommy?"

"He won't be home for dinner," I said. "He told

me to tell you he's meeting Cindy at the mall and having dinner with her."

"So that means we'll be asleep when he gets home, and he'll be asleep when we go to work. I never thought the day would come when I had to make an appointment to see my own son. Especially not when he's living under the same roof," my father said irritably. "Well, I'm just going to leave him a note and invite him — formally — to join us for dinner tomorrow evening. I suppose he slept all day, too?" my father grumbled as he followed me out to the driveway, where he'd pushed the gas grill.

"He only slept until three," I said.

"I'd call that all day, wouldn't you?"

"But he didn't get home until six-thirty," I pointed out.

My father is an accountant. Usually he only gets grumpy around tax time. But that's another thing that's happened since my mother went back to work. Now it seems as if tax time is all year. My mother says his grouchiness is just middle age, along with the pressure of having a college-age son, and that he'll outgrow it. But I think it's because he has to clean the upstairs bathroom and do the vacuuming now that my mother is working.

My father watched silently as I turned on the

gas grill, then poked the fire wand in among the coals. I flicked the igniter, and a row of blue-and-orange flames sprang up. My mother came out with three thick steaks.

"So Buck was here today?" she asked.

"Yeah," I said.

"What did you kids do?"

"We just hung around," I said. I saw her exchange a worried glance with my father, and I knew that wasn't a good enough answer. "We talked about stuff," I added quickly.

"You know we trust you, Roger," my mother said, avoiding my eyes as she carefully set the steaks on the grill. "But young people have a tendency to get into trouble if they don't have enough to occupy them."

"We're occupied," I said quickly.

"It still worries me," my mother went on. "You know I love working. Your father and I want you and Tommy to have a good life and nice things. I was just wondering if maybe I should ask Mrs. Lingreen to look in on you a couple of times a day. Or you could check in with her. I know she'd be delighted to do it."

"Mrs. Lingreen!" I cried. Mrs. Lingreen lives two doors down. She's a retired schoolteacher, and she's been retired for as long as I can remember, so she must be about eighty years old. She's fussy about her yard, and whenever I go there to shovel her out in the winter, she always stands like a police officer, frowning as she watches me from the front window. She's afraid I might miss one flake.

"I don't want that driveway to ice over," she always tells me. Then she has me come in for hot chocolate and graham crackers.

Now I looked at my mother as if she were crazy. "Mom, believe me, Buck, Gina, Lizzie, and I are not going to get into any trouble. Just because we're not in school doesn't mean we're going to go nuts."

To my relief, my father gave her a peculiar look, too.

"Oh, I know," she said with an embarrassed little laugh. "And I know Tommy's not around very often for you either."

"I don't think you have too much to worry about, Joan," my dad said, putting his arm around my shoulder. "Roger's never done anything to disappoint us before. No reason he should start now just because he's on his own a bit more."

I shot my dad a grateful glance. "However," he went on, "if you are looking for things to do this summer, that upstairs bathroom can always use a good cleaning. And you know how to run the vacuum cleaner, don't you, Roger?"

"Come on, Dad," I protested. "Those are your jobs. I do the basement, the yard, and the trash." But I was laughing, too. It was good to see my dad could still kid around. Maybe he was getting used to the idea that my mother was working. And pretty soon, when they saw what a hit our luncheonette was going to be, I was convinced they wouldn't have to worry about how my summer was being occupied, either.

The next morning Buck arrived at eight-thirty. His round, ruddy face was grinning like a clown's. Magic marker spots dotted the front of his worn, white T-shirt. He acted as excited as a little kid on his way to the circus. The reason for his glee was what he modestly called "the brilliance of my advertising campaign."

"Wait until you see what I've created!" he exclaimed. He was carrying some sort of huge sign wrapped in a big green plastic garbage bag. "By the way, you owe me a dollar fifty for materials," he told me.

"You can't just go off spending money without clearing it with us first," I told him as I started upstairs to my room, showing off by taking three steps at a time. Buck followed me, taking only two steps at a time. "Remember, we're supposed to vote on that stuff."

“There isn’t always time,” he argued. “When a creative urge hits you, you have to go with it. You can’t wait around to vote on it. Besides,” he said, “you’re going to love this.”

We closed the door to my room, and he pulled away the plastic to reveal a huge white sign. “Our menu,” he announced. “Listen to the sandwiches. The Totally Nuts — that’s peanut butter with no jelly. Nuts and Jolts — that’s peanut butter with jelly. Full of Bologna, and Loony Tuna. Whaddya think? Will the little kids love it or will they love it?”

I had to smile, because next to each sandwich Buck had drawn a silly, colorful character, giving the sign a really wild cartoon look. Buck could be pretty clever.

The doorbell rang, and I started to answer it. “I think it’s great, but we’ll still have to vote,” I said. “But I’ll vote for you, so there’s half the votes on your side already.”

Gina and Lizzie were waiting outside. Gina was empty-handed, but Lizzie was pulling a brown bag out of her knapsack when they came in. “Buck and I made a test batch of cookies last night,” she announced, heading upstairs. “They’re pretty good, if I do say so myself.”

I followed the girls, eager to make my own decision about the cookies. “Here,” Lizzie said, when the four of us were assembled in my room. She opened the bag and took out four round cookies, each the size of a hearty pancake with a generous sprinkling of M&M's poking through the top.

"I can see it now," Buck declared. "Mighty Monster M&M Cookies — a two-headed ogre with M&M features. I saved a place on the sign just for this." Taking a huge bite, he added, "As delicious this morning as they were last night!"

"They're wonderful, Lizzie," Gina said, her bright pink lipstick fading away as she licked the cookie crumbs from her lips.

"Outstanding," I chimed in. And for a few seconds we all just sat around munching on Lizzie's cookies. Finally I said, "We've got to get down to business. Today we have to shop and put up the signs. I think we should all ride our bikes to the Grand Union together. We'll need all four knapsacks to carry the stuff back here. We can store it in my room and start setting up first thing tomorrow."

For a change, there was no dissent. But a half hour later, after plastering our signs all over the neighborhood, the four of us stood in the peanut butter aisle arguing over which jar to buy.

"Nutty Spread, of course," Gina said. "Look, everyone knows Nutty Spread makes the best peanut butter. And the eighteen-ounce jars are on sale this week. Only $1.79."

"I prefer Peanut Plus," Buck said. "And food is one thing I know a lot about." He patted his round stomach to prove his point.

"So do I." Lizzie agreed. "Consumer tests have shown Peanut Plus is smoother, so it spreads easier. And it tastes better. I wouldn't feed my family anything else," she mimicked.

"Besides," Buck said. "We're not going to buy the eighteen-ounce jars anyway. We need the thirty-two-ounce size. And they're all the same price."

I didn't say so, but I was eyeing the generic brand, which was about half the price of the others and had a plain black-and-white label. According to my father, most generic brands are just as good as the big name brands. They just don't have the fancy labels — which cost more money to make, he always reminds me.

"But Nutty Spread tastes a hundred times better," Gina insisted.

"Well then let's vote," Lizzie said, pushing back her thick brown hair impatiently. "I vote for Peanut Plus."

"Me too," Buck chimed in.

"Sorry, Gina," I said, reaching for two huge jars

of Peanut Plus. Our peanut butter debate was becoming a shopping hazard. A couple of young mothers, with toddlers struggling to get out of their grocery cart seats, gave each other annoyed looks and glared at us as they tried to push their way through the peanut butter aisle. There was no time to consider a tie vote.

"Look," Gina said. "Instead of voting on everything we buy, let's divide the list into four parts. Everyone can use their own judgment. This is going to take forever otherwise." She was already pulling a notebook out of her pocket. "I'll just jot down four separate lists," she explained.

"Who's got the money?" Buck asked.

"I do," I said. Even though Gina was Head of Budget, we'd decided to keep the money at my house since that was our headquarters. "We can meet at the checkout and go through together when we're done. Then I'll pay for it all at once."

"Sounds good," Lizzie said, accepting her assignment from Gina and heading off to find a cart. Buck shook his head, rolled his eyes, and grimaced as he went off. I trailed behind Gina. She had assigned me to paper goods.

"I'm not buying any brand names," I said as we both reached for our carts. "I'm getting everything in generic brands. Black-and-white. It's cheaper, and with paper stuff it's just going to get thrown away anyhow."

Gina only shrugged in a disinterested way, nothing like her usual enthusiastic style. "I'm surprised they didn't buy generic peanut butter," she finally said, haughtily heading down the bread aisle. "I can't believe I'm actually friends with people who eat Peanut Plus."

I looked after her in amazement. Who would ever have guessed that Gina, whose biggest concern in life some days appeared to be lip gloss and nail polish, could have such strong feelings about peanut butter? You certainly learned a lot about people when you went into business with them, I decided, heading for the paper goods.

A few minutes later, as I approached the checkout with my cart filled with generic paper bags, napkins, and baggies, I couldn't help but feel proud of the way I'd shopped. By comparison shopping I found a name brand of baggies on sale, and with a coupon left by some kind shopper I was able to save us forty cents.

I was feeling like a true businessperson, when suddenly I heard Buck's voice. It was loud and angry, and it overpowered the quiet hum of the store's activities. "And I'm telling you, we've got the money," Buck was arguing. "We just don't have it with us right now. Our friend . . ." But he was cut off.

"Then let's see the money," I heard a male voice shouting back from the deli section of the store. I turned the corner just in time to see a blue-coated manager in the distance. With one hand on Buck's cart and the other on Gina's, he'd brought them to a halt, with Lizzie not far behind. Other shoppers were watching curiously, the way people do when they see a police car pulling over a speeding driver.

"I'm getting sick and tired of you kids coming in here and filling up carts and then leaving them," the manager was announcing to the entire store. "You're not the first ones to try this little game. And somebody has to put that stuff back. Did that ever occur to you? And that takes time. And in the business world, time is money!"

"We have the money," Buck cried back. "We're buying this stuff!" Even from where I was I could see his ruddy cheeks were turning even rosier in anger.

"Then why can't you show me your cash?" the manager demanded. He was big and bald and was looking threateningly down at Buck.

"I don't have it," Buck explained. "My friend has it."

The manager turned to Gina. "You've got the money?" he asked.

"No," Gina said. "Roger has it. He's off somewhere shopping for — "

"Off somewhere playing scavenger hunt like the rest of you," the manager interrupted again. "So I suggest you start putting those products right back on the shelves where you found them," he bellowed. "I knew once school got out you kids would think you could play games in the grocery store. You can tell your friends Jack Margolis doesn't tolerate games in his store. This is a place of business, not a playground."

Customers, young men, gray-haired women, and the two mothers with the restless toddlers, were nodding approvingly at Mr. Margolis as I approached with my cart full of paper goods.

"And here comes another one," Mr. Margolis declared. Shoppers turned to stare at me. "You can just turn right around and put all those things back where they belong," he ordered. "What kid needs six loaves of bread, ten cans of tuna, and five hundred napkins?" Some of the shoppers watching us laughed. I suppose it did look rather odd.

"I'm buying these things," I said. "And those things and those things and those things," I added, nodding at Gina, Buck, and Lizzie's carts.

"You are, huh? Let's see the money," Mr. Margolis commanded. He gave his admiring audience of shoppers a knowing look to let them know he could tell I was bluffing.

Suddenly I was angry. Why did everyone think that a group of kids couldn't do anything right unless they were strapped to school desks all year long? My mother wanted Mrs. Lingreen to supervise me, and now the store manager assumed we were trying to disrupt his precious business — just because it was summer vacation and we were on our own, not on some supervised school field trip.

"Here," I said. Slowly I reached into my pocket. I carefully pulled out my wallet, held it for a moment, then deliberately began to open it. "How much do you think we owe you?"

"Over fifty," Mr. Margolis said quickly. "Probably close to sixty."

"Will this do?" I asked, trying to sound mature and casual. I pulled out Gina's crisp twenty, Lizzie's two tens, and the four fives I'd contributed.

Buck, Lizzie, and Gina grinned. Mr. Margolis, looking slightly taken aback, only nodded. "Just get into line," he said weakly. He sounded as if he still wasn't convinced we planned to spend the money. "What are you kids going to do with all this stuff anyway?" he asked suspiciously.

"We're going to — " Buck began to explain.

"Never mind," Lizzie cut in. "We don't owe any explanations. All we owe is money." I liked the way she said it. Not rudely, but as if she knew her rights.

"True," I said.

Mr. Margolis shrugged and stepped aside as the checkout clerk began ringing up our purchases. Fifty-two dollars and sixty-eight cents later, we were the legitimate owners of six bulging bags of groceries. "And only four knapsacks!" groaned Buck. "And we've got to get those little milk cartons into the refrigerator fast, before they go sour. But everything will never fit into just four knapsacks." We had moved through the checkout line and now stood at the front of the store. "What are we going to do?"

"I wish the Grand Union delivered," Gina said in a loud voice. We looked like overloaded camels, each of us bearing the bulging hump of our stuffed backpacks. And we still faced two remaining bags of groceries.

"Having a problem?" Mr. Margolis stepped out from his office where he'd been watching.

"Yeah, we're having a problem," I grumbled. The guy was starting to get on my nerves. I had the feeling he wouldn't let up until he'd ruined our day. A little smile played at the edges of his narrow lips.

"You see, Mr. Margolis," Gina said sweetly. "We only brought four knapsacks. And we bought enough food to fill six. If only there was some safe place we could leave these two bags. It would only be for about a half hour. Then two of us could come back and pick up the rest." She smiled at him, and her eyes, which had some sort of blue stuff smeared around them, turned all big and round.

"Hmm," Mr. Margolis rubbed his chin thoughtfully. "Now, if we were in New York City, where I grew up, this wouldn't be a problem. But markets upstate don't deliver."

"That's right," Gina went on wistfully. "We plan to be buying a lot of groceries this summer. It would be lovely to be able to do all our business at your store."

I cringed and looked away. Lovely indeed. It was making me sick to hear her butter up this jerk.

"Well," Mr. Margolis looked around to be sure a few customers were listening. "Seeing as how I did give you people a bit of a hard time earlier, I suppose I could let you leave those extra bags in the office. But only for a half hour. And don't let it become a habit," he warned.

I headed to the parking lot to get my bike, while Gina and Lizzie followed Mr. Margolis back to the office. "What an idiot," I muttered, as Buck and I unlocked our bikes.

"Who, Gina or Mr. Margolis?" he asked.

"Both," I grumbled.

"I think Gina handled him very well," Buck said. "I couldn't have sweet-talked him like that. But we had to put the groceries somewhere."

"I suppose so," I conceded as we pedaled off.

We raced home, unpacked the first load, then rode back to pick up the rest. Mr. Margolis just grunted from behind his desk as we took the remaining two bags and carefully packed them into our knapsacks. Luckily the nylon was well stretched from carrying school books all year. Still, my back was sore when we were finally finished.

By six o'clock that evening, I'd forgotten all about sore backs and the problem with Mr. Margolis. Looking back, they seemed like nothing. After all, the day had flown by, our signs were up, our supplies put away, and we were planning our setup for opening day. It was dinnertime, however, and I was feeling nervous. We had stored most of the food in my bedroom, but the mayonnaise, juice, milk, and bologna we'd put in the refrigerator in the garage. If my mother decided to open it for some reason tonight, we'd be sunk. My father unwittingly came to the rescue.

"In honor of Tommy's homecoming, how about going out for Chinese tonight?" he asked.

"Super!" I cried. "Great idea!"

My mother smiled happily. She likes it when I'm pleased with parental suggestions. Even if she doesn't always understand the reason why.

5

The green numbers on my digital clock read 5:04 when I opened my eyes on Wednesday morning. It was still a little dark outside, but I could hear the shower water running in the bathroom, so I knew my mother was up. Since she started working, my mother gets up at five every morning. That way, she claims, she has a couple of hours to herself to read the papers, pay bills, and write letters without being disturbed.

Of course I knew I couldn't get up. That would arouse too much suspicion, for even though Tommy was The Sleep Champion at home, I wasn't far behind when it came to appreciation of bedrest. The trouble was, I couldn't sleep any longer. The second I woke up my mind began to race with all the details that were involved in pulling off Day One of The Kids' Luncheonette.

From the weather report on the news last night, the day was supposed to be "unreasonably and unseasonably chilly." In a way, though, I figured that could work to our advantage. It would mean more kids were at home, and they might be so bored that their parents would be glad to take them to a new place for lunch.

I had told Gina, Buck, and Lizzie I'd start setting up as soon as my parents left. I'd move things to the side of the garage and put the card tables, where we'd work, in front of the refrigerator. Suddenly my mind began to race with details. We'd need a cash box and some change to start out. Should we wear aprons to look professional? What if my parents decided, for some reason or another, to stay home from work today? Or worse yet, what if nobody showed up for lunch?

By five-thirty I was itching to get up. I had never realized how long it took my mother to get ready for work. Around six I dozed off. I dreamed about little kids taking bites out of peanut-butter-and-jelly sandwiches, and then making horrible faces and spitting them out. "This tastes terrible! I hate it! I want my money back!" they screamed. They whined louder and louder until my brother's bedroom window opened, and he yelled down to the garage, "Give them back their money so I can get some sleep!"

The word *sleep* jolted me awake. It was seven-thirty! I bounded out of bed just in time to see my father's car heading down the street. My mother always left a few minutes before he did. As I got dressed I decided I'd better not share my dream with the others, even though it was still as fresh in my head as if it had really happened.

"Put a little more jelly on those sandwiches," Lizzie instructed Buck. At ten forty-five, a little less than an hour away from the Grand Opening, Lizzie and Buck were in charge of the peanut-butter-and-jelly sandwiches, while Gina and I were busy making the tuna fish and bologna. We were all being careful not to put too much filling in the sandwiches. Gina had pointed out that appearances count, especially in the food industry. Our sandwiches were the neatest-looking ones I'd ever seen.

Apparently Gina believed *personal* appearances counted in the food industry, too. While Buck, Lizzie, and I were wearing T-shirts and jeans, Gina had on a silky-looking pink blouse, black pants, and sandals that made her taller than Buck. Her blonde hair, usually curly, was standing up straight on top, and she had drawn a thin black line on the top of her eyelids. Lizzie told her she looked great; Buck and I didn't say anything.

In a weak moment just seconds after my friends

had arrived that morning, I'd shared my biggest fear. "What if no one comes?" I'd asked.

"Somebody will come," Buck had replied confidently. "When you advertise as thoroughly as we did, people will come just to see what's going on."

"But to be on the safe side," Lizzie had pointed out sensibly, "maybe we ought to make only a few sandwiches. This idea might need time to catch on. Then if we need more as the day goes by, we can whip them up on the spot. That way people will see how fresh they are, too. Besides, in better restaurants you always have to wait a while for your food."

So we decided to start with a dozen peanut butter sandwiches, six tuna, and six bologna. By eleven-twenty the sandwiches were made, bagged, and carefully piled on one of the two card tables I'd brought out from the living room closet. A line of juice and milk cartons stood on the middle shelf of the refrigerator, next to the apples. A plate of wrapped cookies lay next to the cash box, and a pile of brown bags sat waiting to be filled. On the refrigerator door we'd taped a poster Lizzie had created, stating our prices. It read: *1 sandwich + 1 beverage + 1 dessert = 1 dollar.*

At 11:22 I opened the garage door and looked out. Not a living thing, with the exception of a couple of squirrels, was in sight. Did squirrels eat leftover peanut butter sandwiches, I wondered?

At 11:23 a small black car pulled up at the end of the driveway. A red-headed woman I'd never seen before and two small kids got out. "Is this the lunch place?" she called uncertainly.

"Yep!" I answered enthusiastically, as Buck, Lizzie and Gina echoed the same reply. Quickly we took our places, Buck and Lizzie with the sandwiches, Gina taking care of beverages and desserts, and me behind the cash box.

"All for a dollar?" the woman asked as she read the sign on the refrigerator.

"That's right," Lizzie said. "Sandwich, beverage, and dessert."

"Then we'll have two peanut butter and jelly — " she began.

"No jelly!" interrupted one of the little kids, whose hair was the same rusty red as his mother's.

"One peanut butter with no jelly and one with," she corrected herself. "Or should I say one Totally Nuts, and one Nuts and Jolts! And I'll try your Loony Tuna. Three apple juices and three of those delightful cookies."

While Lizzie went to work making the plain peanut butter sandwich, Buck took two bags and put a sandwich in each one. He passed the bags to Gina, who put a carton of apple juice and a cookie in each one. Then she handed them to me, and I said, "That will be three dollars, please."

As the red-haired woman opened her wallet and counted out three one-dollar bills, a happy ripple of excitement quivered inside me. It reminded me of how I felt on Christmas Day, the thrill I always felt when I first glimpsed the tree, all lit up with piles of wrapped packages underneath. It also made me think of the framed dollar bill that hung in Sam's. Sam's is the barber shop where my dad takes me to get my hair cut. "That's the first dollar Sam ever made," my dad told me a long time ago.

I glanced over at Buck. His eyes were sparkling. Gina had a big grin on her face, and Lizzie was pointing wildly down the street. Two older girls were heading our way with six young kids in tow, and as my three partners gave silent cheers, I tucked the first dollar we made into my jeans for future framing.

"Is there someplace we can sit and eat?" the red-headed woman asked.

For a second I just stared at her. We hadn't given much thought to where people would eat once they'd gotten their meal. "There's a picnic table in the backyard," I said. "Or you can sit on the lawn."

"The grass will be fine. We're in the mood for a picnic. Just like home," she called as she disappeared around the side of the garage, "only easier."

The two older girls ordered lunches for themselves and their six charges, telling us that they were home from college for the summer and had decided to make money baby-sitting. "This is a great idea," exclaimed the girl the little kids called Kathy, handing me eight dollars.

Her friend, whom the kids called Dao, agreed. "It can be so boring being stuck in the house with these kids from seven to five every day. And we don't have a car. Now we can go out for lunch every day. Are you going to be open all summer?"

"It looks that way," I said. Because behind the college girls came two more mothers with small children, a skinny blond boy all alone except for his dog, and four black girls whom I recognized as sixth-graders from school.

After that things began to happen so fast that the time passed in a blur. Kids and adults lined up for lunch, and the only way I could keep up with the constant line was to concentrate totally on the money. Once I looked up and saw that our front yard seemed to have vanished. In its place were people sitting on the grass, eating. Every time I tried to catch Buck, Lizzie, or Gina's eyes, they were too involved in their work to look up. I knew the cash box was filling up fast, and I knew

Lizzie's cookies were steadily disappearing. Last night Lizzie and Buck had made seventy-five cookies; so far only three people had asked for apples.

One of the apple-eaters was Mrs. Lingreen. She appeared at noon and asked for a half a tuna sandwich and an apple. "I'll take it home and have it with my iced tea," she told me. I started to charge her less, but she insisted on a dollar. "You've never taken a cent from me for shoveling my driveway," she told me in her soft, whispery voice. "Besides, I like seeing young people being enterprising." Then she dropped a dollar on the table and walked back home.

At twelve forty-five, with just fifteen minutes to closing, a blue van pulled up, and a plump bald man with four plump boys got out. The boys raced hungrily ahead of their father up the driveway.

"I want a tuna fish on rye," the first one demanded. I recognized him from school, a loudmouthed kid named Jeff Waters who was always in trouble and spent most of his recess time in the detention room.

"Do you mean a Loony Tuna? We don't have rye bread," Lizzie said. "But I can give you some extra tuna fish."

"Forget it," Jeff said. "Just give me two cookies and two grape juices instead. For a dollar," he added.

"I'm sorry," Lizzie said politely. "No substitutions are allowed. As you can see, the sign says 1 sandwich + 1 beverage + 1 dessert = 1 dollar."

"How much if you don't want a sandwich?" Jeff countered. His brothers, two of whom were third-grade twins and the other a round, kindergarten version of the older boys, clustered around the cookies.

"Still a dollar," Lizzie said crisply.

"That's not fair," Jeff snarled.

Mr. Waters strode up to the table. "Gimme three bologna sandwiches, and one peanut butter, and one tuna, and five grape juices, and five of them cookies."

"But I don't want a sandwich," Jeff whined.

"So don't eat it," his father said. "It comes with the deal, so we take it."

Buck filled five bags with the sandwiches and dropped in the juices. But when he passed the last bag to Gina she said apologetically, "Sorry, we only have four cookies left. Will an apple do?"

"No," Jeff said flatly. "You don't want no apple, do ya, Dad?"

"No way," Mr. Waters declared.

For a moment no one spoke. We hadn't made any plans for dealing with angry customers, and I was beginning to realize how lucky we'd been until now.

Fortunately our luck held out a few seconds longer. It was the littlest Waters boy who saved us from his father's dissatisfaction. "I want an apple," he announced. "My teacher says they're 'nature's toothbrush.' Candy gives you holes in your teeth."

Mr. Waters seemed almost disappointed by this display of good sense in his youngest son. "Ya sure?" he grumbled.

"Yep," said the boy.

Grudgingly, Mr. Waters took the last four cookies and an apple, and we watched with relief as the family drove off.

Then Buck ran into the house. Seconds later he returned with a new sign. It read: CLOSED. Quickly we taped it to the garage door. We lowered the door and stood for a silent second surveying The Kids' Luncheonette — minus the kids. We were out of cookies and down to our last two juices. My front yard was littered with napkins and baggies, the garage was a mess, and although the cash box was overflowing, I knew most of the money would have to go back into buying tomorrow's supplies.

But we were ecstatic! We began to whoop. "We did it!" Buck cried, raising his plump hands together in a tight clasp above his head.

"We did it without a hitch!" Lizzie chimed in.

"It's a winner!" Gina screamed.

"We're rich!" I yelled, throwing the pile of dollar bills up in the air like confetti.

Then I happened to glance over at the kitchen door. Standing in the doorway was a sleepy-looking seventeen-year-old, and at that moment no one in her right mind would have called him *cute*.

"What in the world do you guys think you're doing?" Tommy demanded. His mustache seemed to have grown darker overnight. Or maybe it was just the way he asked us what we were doing. Because he didn't really *ask* us—he *growled* at us.

6

Our joyous yelps were shut off like a radio by the sight and sound of Tommy. He was still in his pajamas, and his eyes had a half-awake glaze that made him look ferocious.

"Uh . . . we're . ." I stammered, not knowing exactly where to begin. I wanted to make things look as good as possible to Tommy, because I sure wasn't going to back out of the luncheonette now. And I knew we'd need Tommy's support to continue. For a second I wondered if he could be bought. But as I tried to come up with a convincing explanation, I forgot one vital piece of information: Tommy could read.

"Totally Nuts?" he remarked, studying Buck's colorful sign which hung on the refrigerator. "That sounds like you guys all right. And so do Nuts and Jolts, Full of Bologna, and Loony Tuna.

What is this, some kind of whacky restaurant game you're playing?"

"It's not a game," Lizzie said defensively. "It's a successful business. We're running a kids' luncheonette."

"*Successful* is right," Buck chimed in. "Look at these profits." He pointed to the overflowing cash box. "And listen, Tommy," he added, "have a sandwich or an apple. On the house. We're sorry if we woke you up."

One thing I can say for Buck, when it comes to public relations he's a natural. Unfortunately, I knew by my brother's look of disgust that he wasn't in the mood for one of our leftover bologna sandwiches.

"I suppose Mom and Dad have given you their permission to turn the garage into a fast-food store?" Tommy asked, ignoring everyone else and turning his icy glare directly on me. "I suppose it just slipped their minds to tell me all about it?"

"Not really," I said weakly. "This is only the first day. I didn't want to get them all excited until I was sure it would work."

"They'll be excited all right," Tommy said. "Wow, will they ever be excited."

"Come on, Tommy," I pleaded, "give us a chance."

"We'll keep the house quiet for you," Buck chimed in. "We were just celebrating the triumphant end of our first day. It won't happen again, we promise."

Tommy gave Buck a cool look as he padded toward the refrigerator in his bare feet. He opened it up to survey our stock. "Mind if I have a juice?" he asked. "After all, I am fully awake two hours earlier than usual."

"Have two," Lizzie said sarcastically. "One for each hour." She was standing up very straight and looked ready to take Tommy on.

Tommy shot her a nasty glance as he poked the plastic straw into the juice carton and took a long sip. I got the feeling she didn't think he was the least bit cute anymore.

Actually, my brother is a good guy. And the juice seemed to make him feel a bit more human. "Look," he said. "I don't care what you do. As long as you do two things. First: don't wake me up again. And second: tell Mom and Dad. I'm not taking any responsibility for whatever messes you're going to get yourselves into this summer. Got it?"

"Sure," I said. "As I told you before, I was planning on telling them. Tonight. As soon as they get home. Before dinner, I'm going to tell them the whole thing."

"Bright idea," Tommy said. He finished off the juice in a single noisy slurp. "Not bad," he said, looking directly at Lizzie. "In fact, I will have two."

"Go ahead," Buck said, trying to sound jovial as Tommy pulled another juice from the refrigerator. "Enjoy yourself."

"See you later tonight," Tommy said to me as he headed back inside. "I can't wait to see how Mom and Dad feel about living in a real live luncheonette."

"They'll be glad," I said, with as much conviction as I could muster, as he disappeared behind the kitchen door.

But as we cleaned up I wasn't so sure. "Maybe we should hold off buying any more supplies until I clear this with my parents," I suggested to the partners.

"We can't do that," Buck argued. "We won't have time to shop and get everything ready by noon tomorrow."

"Make it eleven," Gina corrected. "You're forgetting how early some people eat lunch. Especially kids. Besides, I promised Lizzie and Buck I'd help with the cookies tonight. That's going to take a while. So I'll want to sleep in tomorrow. Not that real sleep is even possible with that colicky baby in the house."

“This is a business, Gina,” I said. “We can’t be worrying about sleep when there are important decisions to be made. Let’s vote. How many think we should wait until tomorrow to shop again?”

But the truth was, I had another reason for putting off the shopping. I, too, was thinking about sleep. Seeing Tommy head back upstairs to his room had made me think of my own bed. The idea of lugging in groceries from the Grand Union didn’t thrill me.

“I vote we shop now,” Lizzie said briskly. “Not only should we have our supplies ready, but when your parents see that everything is bought, they’ll have to let you go ahead with it. Besides, this is a business venture. In business you take chances.”

“I agree,” Gina echoed.

“Me, too,” Buck said. “But let’s count the money first.”

It turned out we’d taken in sixty-one dollars. When we figured it out, we’d spent fifty-three dollars on groceries and three dollars on advertising, so our profit for the day was five dollars.

“That’s a dollar twenty-five each,” Lizzie said. “Not bad for the first day.” Everyone else seemed satisfied, so I didn’t say anything. But to me, a dollar-twenty-five seemed like a pretty small amount for all the work we’d done.

As soon as the garage and yard were back in

order, with every crumb swept away, every napkin tucked out of sight, and all the signs stored in my room, the four of us headed off again to the Grand Union. This time, however, the shopping went more quickly. Without even having to discuss it, we all set off to get our share of the groceries. As I hurried down the paper goods aisle I saw Mr. Margolis ahead stacking a display of facial tissue. He looked up when he saw me coming. "You kids still buying groceries?" he asked me in a teasing voice. "I've got some nice facial tissue on sale here."

"No, thanks," I said, dropping a jumbo box of sandwich bags and a hundred generic brown paper bags into my cart.

"Have a nice day," Mr. Margolis said as I wheeled the cart away.

"Thanks," I grumbled. I had a feeling he was trying to be friendly. And so far, my day had been better than nice. But now I was feeling tired and worried. What could I say to my parents to convince them to let me continue with the luncheonette, I wondered, as I passed frozen foods and headed to the checkout. Ahead I saw Buck, Gina, and Lizzie already standing in line. For a second I studied their faces. Like mine, they all looked tired, and Gina was giving a slow, wide yawn. But something in the way they were standing there, proud and determined, made me remember how just a couple of days ago we'd all been hanging around, bored and complaining. We sure weren't bored or complaining now. And thinking of that, I knew I had to come up with some way to convince my parents to let us continue.

At six-fifteen my mother's voice calling, "Dinner, Roger!" woke me from a weird dream where Mr. Margolis and I were all dressed up in three-piece suits, piling stacks of quarters as high as the facial tissue display I'd seen him working on today. I was starving, and as I hurried down to dinner I tried to remember if I'd eaten lunch myself. In the crazy whirl of our first day I realized I hadn't.

My parents were in the kitchen. My mother was poking around in the refrigerator when I came in. My father was sitting at the kitchen table with a peculiar look on his face, sipping a glass of tonic water and not looking directly at me. "Hi," I said as nonchalantly as I could.

From the refrigerator came a muffled "Hi" from my mother. My father just nodded. My mother emerged from the refrigerator clutching a head of lettuce and two green peppers and gave my father a sharp look.

"So, how did you spend your day today, Roger?" my father asked me.

Right then I should have told them. But the words wouldn't come. "Oh, Buck, Lizzie, and Gina came over," I said. "We hung out. We — "

"I bought this tonic at the Price Chopper," my father interrupted. "It was on sale. I bought a case of it." He looked at me pointedly. "It was a sensible buy."

I was suddenly baffled. Something was going on. My father was trying to tell me something, but what it was, I couldn't figure out. "That's good, Dad," I said. "I'm glad you got a good buy."

"You know, Roger, when things are on sale, or seem to be inexpensive, we only buy them if we need them. Or if we're sure they'll last until we can use them."

I nodded. "Like this tonic water," my father went on. "It can stay fresh and tasty a long time."

"Waste is a terrible thing," my mother said. "People are hungry in this world. That's why I don't like to throw away food."

Now I was completely lost. "Yeah, me, too," I said.

"Then why did you buy all that bologna, mayonnaise, apples, milk, and heaven knows what else you've got stashed away around here! And in the middle of the week, without asking if we needed it? I know you want to be helpful, Roger. And I appreciate it. But try to be sensible, too!"

It all came together in a flash. My father, when he put his case of tonic in the old refrigerator, had seen our supplies. "I *am* being sensible," I said. "Honest. Just ask Tommy."

"But why?" my mother wailed. "Why would you buy so much bologna and tuna fish? Those apples will go bad. And you don't even like apples. So who's going to eat it all? And where did you get the money?"

"I'm running a luncheonette," I said quietly.

My parents looked at me as if I had suddenly started singing in fluent Chinese. "A luncheonette?" my father asked.

"Lizzie, Buck, Gina, and I put our money together and started a business," I said. I detected a faint interest in their expressions, so I quickly went on. "Today was our first day, and it went off without a hitch. I was going to tell you tonight, really. Tommy said I had to. I was just waiting for the right time."

My parents kept glancing at each other with looks I couldn't quite read. "It's not anything dangerous," I finally pleaded. "And it's not illegal. Remember, you said kids get into bad stuff when they don't have anything better to do."

It was true; running the luncheonette wouldn't leave us time to get into trouble.

"You know," my father said thoughtfully, "I think Roger does have a point. When you think about it, there's not an awful lot for kids Roger's age to do around here in the summer. Especially with the weather so rotten. At twelve they're still too young to get real jobs and too old to go to camp. Maybe a business venture for the summer isn't such a bad idea."

I could hardly believe my ears. "Do you mean it?"

"I mean, I'll give it serious consideration," my father said. "Your mother and I are responsible for what happens here. I don't want the neighbors complaining."

"We're only open for an hour and a half," I explained. "Mostly people just stop by, pick up their lunches and go off somewhere to eat it. But they really seemed to like it! Over fifty people came by — even Mrs. Lingreen," I added, hoping to please my mother.

"You must have done quite a job cleaning up," she said reluctantly. "If your father hadn't found the food, I never would have known half the neighborhood had lunch here today."

"Then you'll let us keep doing it?" I asked.

Again my parents exchanged glances. I could tell they weren't convinced.

"I think we'll take it day by day," my father said. "I can't make any blanket promises. One day I'm going to stop by for one of your lunches myself. I want to see how this operation runs before I make any drastic decisions."

"You'll see," I promised. "Drop by any day. We have nothing to hide."

"You have to promise me no one will be coming into the house," my mother said.

"I promise."

"And that if you have any problems you'll come to us and tell us — immediately," my father added. "You may not believe this, Roger," he said, sounding a little gruff, "but we don't want to work against you. We want to work with you."

"Yeah, I know," I said, relieved.

Suddenly I felt this funny lump starting in my throat. It was relief, mixed with a new feeling. For the first time in my life I actually felt a little sorry for my parents. I mean, here they were letting me keep this luncheonette going and even offering to help me, when I knew perfectly well it wasn't exactly what they wanted to have in their garage.

"So I can tell the other guys it's okay to come over tomorrow?" I asked.

"Yes," my mother said.

"Day by day," my father reminded me as I started for the phone.

"Dinner's in five minutes," my mother called.

But dinner suddenly didn't seem terribly important. It was only lunch that mattered.

Our second business day got off to a slow start. The weather was cooperating once again — it was gray and chilly — but by noon it still looked like no one in the neighborhood was ready to eat.

"Maybe we should offer soup," Gina suggested, shivering as she stood behind the card table piled high with sandwiches.

"Maybe you shouldn't wear a bathing suit when it's cold out," Buck grumbled, looking anxiously down the empty street.

"This is not a bathing suit," Gina retorted, tugging at the sleeveless yellow shirt she had on. "It's my new tank top, which happens to match these running shorts perfectly. I think it's important to look fresh and summery when you are in a summer business."

"But aren't you freezing?" Lizzie asked. She had on jeans and a pink sweatshirt that said IF

YOU THINK I'M CUTE YOU SHOULD SEE MY GRANDMOTHER.

"No," Gina said. "I'm refreshed. And once we start working I'll probably be the most comfortable. You guys are all overdressed. Besides, when the sun comes out you'll all be sweating while I'll be able to work on my tan."

"If you haven't turned blue in the meantime," Buck said sharply.

"Did you know that pigs are the only animals besides humans that can get sunburned?" Lizzie asked, trying to change the subject. "I read it in the newspaper last night."

Like me, she could feel a fight starting between Buck and Gina. That was something we didn't need. So I was glad to spot the two baby-sitting girls from yesterday coming up the driveway with their flock of small kids behind them.

"Look," I said. "Repeat customers. Always a good sign in business." Buck and Gina forgot their differences and fell into their work positions. "Hi," I said to Kathy and Dao. "What can we get you today?"

"I want a cookie," yelled one of the little boys. He looked about four years old.

"They've been bugging us all morning to come back here for lunch," Dao said with a laugh. "They think it's a big deal to go out to eat."

Kathy laughed, too, and ordered eight lunches. As we scrambled to fill the order I saw Mr. Waters' bald head leaning out of his van as he tried to park it before his boys all clambered out. I checked the cookie tray. Seeing it was full, I relaxed. Today there would be no bickering with Mr. Waters.

As I started to get ready for them, two new groups started up the driveway. A mother and two little girls came behind three kids I'd never seen before. For the next few minutes all I said was, "That will be two dollars, please." Or, "That's three dollars. Yes, we can change a twenty."

Then I felt Lizzie slip up next to me and give me a solid poke on the arm. "Look who's here," she whispered. I glanced up from the cash box just in time to see Victoria Chubb swing one long leg off a shiny green European twelve-speed bicycle, which she casually leaned against the side of my house. I felt all the partners' eyes following her as she slowly walked into the garage and gave an appraising look around.

Victoria Chubb is no taller than I am. But something about the way she carries herself, the way she holds her head so that her thick black curls never move, makes her seem not only a lot bigger than me, but a lot older.

"Ignore her," I whispered to Lizzie. How easily I had forgotten that Victoria, with her pushy way of acting as if she's an authority on every subject in the world, is a very difficult person to ignore.

"Right," Lizzie said, dropping a tuna fish sandwich into a bag and passing it on to Buck for a cookie and a carton of milk.

"What can I get you, Victoria?" It was Gina, undaunted, who invited Victoria to place an order.

Ignoring Gina, Victoria stepped up to the table across from me. As if she lived here, she gave the table a small, approving pat. "Nice operation, Roger," she said. "Very nice indeed."

"Thanks. We think so," I said. I did not want to discuss my "operation" with Victoria. I did not want her in my garage. But I didn't want any trouble from her, either.

"You've got the basics down well," she went on, her small dark eyes surveying the food we had out, the signs, and the piles of baggies and napkins. Victoria has smooth, pale skin, so pale that her eyes look almost black against it, even though they're really dark brown. She probably could be pretty. But the way she acts ruins it. Now I saw her dark brown eyes linger on the cash box. "You breaking even yet?"

"Yes," I said proudly. "In fact, we each made over a dollar yesterday."

"Well that's not very much," Victoria informed me. "Are you doing this for your health, or for a profit?"

"Very funny, Victoria," I replied. "The summer's not over yet. Just wait. We'll make a lot of money."

"Not if you're barely breaking even now," Victoria told me smugly. "Unless you have plans to expand — which I guess you don't — you're going to see when the novelty wears off, your business will take a plunge."

"We already have regular customers," I told her. Who did she think she was, coming in here and telling us what was going to happen to our luncheonette? And why wasn't anyone else speaking up to her?

"Regulars are a good foundation," Victoria conceded. "But I've done a lot of work studying companies and businesses. Actually, I've become an expert on business. You're going to need a consultant before the summer is through. I've just dropped by to offer my services."

"I thought you were going to camp." To my relief, Lizzie had finally spoken up.

"Not until the last week in August," Victoria informed her. "I'll be available to consult until then."

"We don't need a consultant," Buck said. "The

four of us are equal partners. We can handle things just fine. We vote on everything anyway."

"What happens if it's two against two?" Victoria asked. "What you need is another partner. Someone who knows the inside track of business. Someone like me."

I heard Gina give a slight gasp. But she needn't have worried. If Victoria Chubb thought we'd ever vote her in as a fifth partner, she was really off in outer space.

"I could show you how to maintain your consistency, while at the same time changing with the needs of your customers," Victoria continued, a little too smoothly. It sounded like a line she'd memorized from somewhere. "For investment camp I've been doing a lot of research. Why, I could probably double your business in a week."

"We like our business just the way it is," I said. "Now what do you want for lunch, Victoria? There are more customers coming. We don't have time to stand around and talk."

Victoria Chubb gave me a vicious glare. I guess she didn't like being brushed off. "I'd like to see your license," she snapped. "My Uncle Phil just happens to be a restaurant inspector for the county, and it so happens you have to have a license to serve food. And you have to be inspected, too."

My mind froze. I couldn't think of a thing to say. Something told me Victoria knew what she was talking about.

Somehow Lizzie came to my rescue again. "We're working on it," she said, giving Victoria a direct look. "We're not as inexperienced as you think." Even though she sounded cool, I knew Lizzie had to be as astonished as I was. We'd never considered the thought that we might need a *permit* to serve food.

"Well, you'd better work on it fast," Victoria retorted. "Because my uncle is very close to me. He's around a lot in the summer. So one of these days I think I'll bring him here for lunch."

"Fine," said Lizzie. "We serve everyone."

"After he finds the violations, you only get warned once," Victoria continued. "Then he can drop by any time and close you down. And without a permit he can close you down any old time he feels like it."

"Have a bologna sandwich, Victoria," Buck interrupted. "You're so full of it now a little more won't matter."

"I happen to be an *expert* when it comes to making money," Victoria said indignantly. "Since I have other stops to make, I'm afraid I don't have much time for lunch. But I'll leave you my card.

And I'll be back with my Uncle Phil to have a meal here. Soon."

From her pants pocket Victoria pulled out a small white piece of cardboard. She dropped it on the table, then headed to her bike. As she pedaled off, I picked up the card. VICTORIA CHUBB it read. BUSINESS CONSULTANT. It also gave Victoria's address and phone number, and I suspected it was one of a kind, something Victoria had just typed up that morning.

"What an idiot," Buck said, turning his attention to a group of fourth-grade neighborhood boys who looked like they'd just broken up their softball game to come for lunch. But even Buck sounded a little uncertain. I figured he had to be wondering about the permit, too.

"I can't believe her nerve," Lizzie said. "She's all talk."

But for a change I didn't agree with Lizzie. Victoria Chubb made me uneasy. Some of the things she said, things I never would have thought of, made sense. And I suspected Victoria, for all her talk, didn't lie. Which meant if she really did have an uncle who was a restaurant inspector, we could be in for big trouble.

But there was no time to worry now. A line was forming in front of us, and for the rest of the lunch hour we were busy making lunches.

7

Monday and Tuesday of the following week, business remained pretty steady. My parents asked a few questions each night, then talked about other stuff. I think they wanted me to know that they trusted me and they weren't going to make a fuss over the luncheonette — unless something went wrong. My dad dropped in one day for lunch, complimented us on the tasty tuna fish, then said he had to hurry back to the office for a meeting. No big deal.

So far I hadn't told my parents about Victoria Chubb and her uncle, the restaurant inspector. I figured there was no reason to bring it up until he actually came in with a clipboard and started poking around. And there'd been no sign of Victoria since she pedaled off on her twelve-speed, leaving us holding her business card. But the bitter memory of her visit stayed with me.

Then on Wednesday the weather turned warm

and, like the well-known bad penny, Victoria turned up again. She came riding up the driveway at twelve-fifty, took one look around, glanced at our faces, and said smugly, "What did I tell you? It looks like business is off today."

Unfortunately, she was right. For the past couple of days the profits had been dropping — just by a few dollars or a couple of extra cookies left over. But this day had been our all-time low. Each night we made seventy-five cookies. Today a pile of at least thirty-five still sat, wrapped and ready to be bought, which meant instead of our usual seventy-five to eighty customers, we'd had only about forty. And there was no one in sight to buy any more.

"It's the weather," Buck replied. "People are going away — or to the pool." His blue T-shirt was sticking to his back, and even though he had on shorts, his ruddy face was sweaty.

"McDonald's survives warm weather," Victoria retorted. "So do Burger King and Wendy's. Want me to tell you how?"

"How?" Gina asked wearily, looking up from her seat by the cash box. She'd claimed she'd only had five hours of sleep last night, so we'd told her she could take the money sitting down. Today Gina looked cool but tired.

"Are you still serving?" Victoria asked. "I'd like

a plain jelly sandwich, juice, and a cookie. What flavors of juice do you have?"

Lizzie opened the refrigerator to display our juice selection, while Buck grudgingly turned to make the jelly sandwich. We didn't get too many requests for those, but that was Victoria. Always a little bit different.

"What you people need," Victoria began slowly, a big frown covering her face as she acted as if she were almost in pain from concentration, "what you need is a gimmick. You need a gimmick to attract new business and excite your regular customers."

"That will be one dollar," I said crisply, handing her a full lunch bag.

"What kind of gimmick?" Buck asked, as Victoria reached over absently to pay me. With a twenty-dollar bill!

"We can't change this!" I cried. "Come on, Victoria. Don't you have anything smaller?"

"No," she said innocently, taking a huge bite out of her jelly sandwich.

I wanted to reach across the table and snatch the sandwich out of her hand. If Victoria Chubb imagined for one second that because we didn't have nineteen dollars in change she'd be getting a free lunch, we had news for her. But that didn't seem to be what she had in mind. "Just give me whatever you can," she said. "You can owe me the rest."

Something in this smelled fishy. I wasn't going to owe Victoria Chubb anything.

"No way," I said. "We don't want to start owing anybody. The next time you come by you can pay for it." This way Victoria would owe *us*.

"Whatever you say," Victoria said, tucking the twenty-dollar bill casually into her jeans pocket.

"I'll make a note of this to put in the cash box," Lizzie said. "One lunch charged to the account of Victoria Chubb."

"What's your interest rate for a charge account?" Victoria asked.

Lizzie looked at her with annoyance. "Just pay us by the end of the week," she snapped.

Victoria only smirked as she took another bite of her sandwich.

It was nearly one o'clock. "I'm calling a business meeting in my room at one-fifteen," I announced. "Let's start cleaning up now."

Buck got the CLOSED sign, and we began sweeping, throwing away, and straightening. Because of our low volume it didn't take very long. Suddenly I was discouraged. Maybe it was time to put up an OUT OF BUSINESS sign instead, I thought, as I stored the rest of the cookies in the refrigerator.

"Better luck tomorrow," Victoria called as she slid onto her shiny new leather seat. "You've got my card if you need me," she reminded us, one hand on the handle bars and the other still clutching her juice carton. Forget the OUT OF BUSINESS sign, I decided, making a nasty face at the back of her curly head. We'd show her. The Kids' Luncheonette wasn't bankrupt yet. And we had no need for the services of a consultant!

The business meeting began promptly at one-fifteen. It was disappointing to be able to eat as many leftover cookies as we wanted, but we did anyway. "I think we're heading into a slump," Buck said, picking out a yellow M&M. He was sitting on the floor next to Lizzie — and the cookies. "And I also think having Victoria Chubb around too much is a curse." Crumbs, like grains of sand, were sprinkled around his mouth, as he reached for another cookie.

"I agree," Gina said from the bed, where she was stretched out. "Remember she said business would drop off? And it has." She stifled a yawn and popped a chunk of cookie into her mouth.

"She also said we needed a gimmick to bring business back," Lizzie reminded us. "She just might be right about that, too."

"What kind of gimmick?" I asked, playing with

a pencil at my desk. "You mean, like someone dressing up as a clown and passing out balloons?"

"Too corny," Buck said. "How about a sale? A ninety-nine cent sale."

"We only charge a dollar now," Lizzie reminded him. "We're giving the food away as it is. We've got to do better than that."

"Maybe we should give away something else," Gina said thoughtfully. "You know, a free juice to the lucky winner who. . . ."

"Who what?" Buck asked.

"Who . . oh, I don't know. Who guesses something, or who gets a sandwich that has something in it."

"Like what?" I asked. "A piece of paper or something?"

"Let me think," Gina said. "When you're as exhausted as I am, thoughts don't come to you very fast."

"Better not take a chance with anyone swallowing something that could hurt them," Lizzie said. Her father's daughter — always looking to avoid lawsuits.

"How about a chocolate chip?" Gina asked. "They're easy to conceal, and cheap."

"Sounds good," I agreed. "We could hide maybe five chips a day in five sandwiches. The winners get a free lunch, good for the next day. That way they have to come back and bring their friends or family with them."

"I like it," Lizzie admitted. "But do you think it's enough? I mean, that might work as a small improvement, but we need one big overall gimmick that everyone can enjoy."

"Sandwiches are not the most exciting things to work with," Buck pointed out. "I mean, what can you do to a sandwich?"

For a few seconds we just sat and pondered that. It was true. Sandwiches — square, soft, pale sandwiches — certainly didn't inspire creativity.

"Whatever we do, it has to be cheap," Lizzie said. "How can you cheaply jazz up a sandwich?"

"Food coloring?" Gina wondered aloud. "Could we dye the bread and have colored sandwiches? I bet the little kids would love that. And we could make them in all shapes and sizes."

"You can't color bread," I said. "Unless you make the dough yourself, and I, for one, am not going to spend my summer baking bread."

"Roger's right," Lizzie agreed. "It's too hot to bake bread, and it takes too long. Besides, little kids like store bread. Not only that, but the thought of green and yellow bread is sickening."

Gina looked insulted. She put her head down and intently began to examine her chipped fingernail polish. "But you may have something when it comes to shapes," Lizzie went on quickly. "We could cut the sandwiches into different shapes. Like bunnies and ducks. The kids would like that, I bet."

"Bunnies and ducks!" Buck exclaimed. "That's the dumbest thing I ever heard of. It's July! Who wants bunnies and ducks in July?"

I nodded in complete agreement. Lizzie's usual common sense was letting us down. "It doesn't have to be seasonal," Lizzie argued. "Think of something that would be year-round."

"The sun," Gina offered. "The sun, the moon, the stars, the planets."

"I can see it now," Buck said laughing. " 'One tuna crescent and one peanut-butter-and jelly big dipper, please.' Count me out on that."

We were getting nowhere, and I could feel an argument brewing. Then suddenly I had an idea. "Just a second," I said, jumping up. Downstairs in the kitchen I knew my mother had a box of old cookie cutters. When I was a kid and at home sick with a cold or the chicken pox, she'd get them out and let me use them to trace and color. I ran downstairs and rifled through drawers until I found the box. Bringing it back to my bedroom, I poured the tinny collection onto my bed. There were a couple dozen cutters, everything from gingerbread men to Valentine hearts. There were dogs, ducks, and a funny-looking Santa. Then I saw them! Vaguely, I remembered my mother had used them when she'd been in a bridge club. She'd ordered special cutters to make sandwiches in the shapes of hearts, clubs, diamonds, and spades. They were bigger than the usual cookie cutters; they eliminated most waste and really only trimmed off the crust. What was left after you pressed down and gently lifted up the cutter, was a sandwich that reminded you of a deck of cards.

"These!" I cried, holding up the heart and diamond shapes. "My mother used them for her bridge club, and when she wanted Tommy and me to have a special lunch or to eat some kind of horrible-tasting sandwich. She'd cut them out with these."

Gina grabbed the club and spade. A splash of excitement colored her cheeks. Her sleepy eyes were suddenly opened wide. "We've got it!" she cried.

Buck jumped and put his hand on his forehead. "A new advertising blitz is coming to life before my very eyes," he declared. "The luncheonette will be renamed — Aces. We'll advertise with new posters. We can decorate them with old decks of cards stapled along the edges. We'll call it 'A

New Concept in Noontime Dining for Youngsters.' This idea is hot. It could be the start of the big-time for us!"

"I love it, too!" Lizzie conceded. "We needed something new — a gimmick — like Victoria said. I think we've got one."

"These cookie cutters are neat," Gina said, examining the heart more closely. "But kids are going to want whatever shape they ask for. How are we going to do this?"

"We'll make the sandwiches as usual," Lizzie said slowly, trying to anticipate any and all snags in this new plan before we got in too far. "Then the kids can ask for a shape, and we'll cut it for them. It'll only take a second."

"And inside five lucky sandwiches there'll be a hidden chocolate chip, right?" Buck asked. He'd grabbed a piece of paper and was already sketching the first signs. "Who's got some old decks of cards we can use?" he asked. "We want to keep the advertising expenses to a minimum."

"Do you think we should raise our prices, too?" Gina asked. "I mean, isn't that what companies do when they come out with something that is new and improved?"

"If we're going to raise prices, now is the time to do it," Lizzie noted. "The increase will go right along with the new advertising campaign."

"But we're in a slump," I pointed out. "It's not the time to raise prices."

"We're not in a slump because we're too expensive," Lizzie said. "We're in a slump because we're stale — if you'll pardon the expression." She looked at her watch. "It's almost two, and we've still got to shop. Let's vote on the price increase."

The vote was three to one. I still wasn't convinced that was the way to go. But as of the next day our lunches were a dollar twenty-five — and The Kids' Luncheonette was renamed Aces.

We spent the rest of the afternoon making up the introductory advertising campaign. Our new name, Aces, had the ring of a winner, we were all convinced of that. For lunch we made ourselves sandwiches: a tuna spade for Buck, a jelly heart for Gina — she insisted on strawberry instead of grape jelly for authenticity — a bologna club for Lizzie and a peanut butter diamond for me. It was weird, but the sandwiches actually seemed to taste better in the shapes. Maybe it was because the crusts were gone, or because we had to fill them a bit less to avoid the sandwiches getting too floppy, but they were lighter and more fun to eat.

Before going to the grocery store that afternoon, we put up our new sign. We'd splurged and bought two packs of fluorescent markers. We outlined the new name and slogan in psychedelic orange, red, and pink, and stapled playing cards along the corners. The result was masterful — if we did say so ourselves.

"We may have to give it a couple of days to catch on," Lizzie warned as we waited to go through the checkout line. "New ideas take time. But I think everyone is going to love it."

"They'd better," I said, looking at our shopping carts and my wallet. Maybe the price increase wasn't such a bad idea after all, I admitted, pulling out the last of our cash to pay for Aces — Phase Two of the Kids' Luncheonette.

The following day I felt more nervous waiting for customers than I had on Opening Day. I think we all did, because this idea of a successful luncheonette had grown on us. It was more than just a way to spend the summer or a way to make money. Now if we succeeded, it meant we knew something more about life than just school and home.

By twelve-fifteen I was feeling pretty good. Customers were in line; little kids were thrilled to be able to eat a sandwich that didn't look like a sandwich. "I don't know what shape to pick, so I want one of each," a tiny blonde girl demanded.

"Have one shape today and a different one tomorrow," her mother told her. Then she turned to me. "Linda's always been a poor eater," she said. "This is the first time I can ever remember her showing such an interest in food. You kids have a great thing going here."

"Thanks," I said as her daughter finally chose a peanut-butter-and-jelly spade. "Don't forget to look for a chip in the sandwich, Linda," I reminded her as she headed off happily with her lunch bag.

Kathy and Dao, our most faithful customers, loved the idea, too. "I want two extra lunches to go," I heard Dao telling Gina. "My boyfriend will love this."

Even the Waters clan was impressed. Mr. Waters ordered a bologna spade for himself and one of each of the shapes for his boys. "Where'd you find those sandwich cutters?" he asked. "Have you got any more you're willing to sell?"

"No, sir," I said. "These are my mother's. I don't know where she got them."

"You ask her, will you?" Mr. Waters said. "Let me know where she got them."

"Sure," I said.

"There's a chip in mine!" One of Dao's charges

rushed up to the table and showed everyone who cared to look a chocolate chip, lying on top of the jelly filling of his sandwich.

"You're a winner!" Gina cried. "The first one today!" She gave him a small certificate for one free lunch, and the four of us gave each other satisfied looks as parents and kids all carefully examined their sandwiches for hidden chips.

By the end of the lunch hour, the other four winners had come forth. Two were new customers, which was a good thing, because it gave them a reason to come back. And the other three were regulars, which was also fine. We wanted our regulars to be happy, too.

Later that afternoon, counting the money in my room, we found we'd finally made a decent profit. Not one person had complained about the extra cost — not even Mr. Waters — and when we figured out what we'd need for groceries the following day, it appeared we had made about ten dollars.

"I am donating this old sneaker box to hold the profits," I announced, bringing forth an empty Adidas high-tops box I'd been saving in my closet for no special reason.

"And what will we do with the profits?" Gina asked.

"The fair thing is to wait until the end of the summer," Lizzie said. "If we set our goal at four hundred dollars and we make it, we can split the profits by four. That will give us one hundred dollars each to do with as we choose."

"One hundred dollars," Gina murmured dreamily. "Back-to-school wardrobe, here I come."

"Wardrobe nothing," Buck said. "I've got my eye on a twelve-speed bike. Did you see Victoria's? *She* may be a jerk. But her bike is terrific!"

"Let's not talk about Victoria Chubb," I said. "Things are going too well now. She's just bad luck."

And for the next couple of days it looked as if all we had to do was just what we were doing. The shaped sandwiches were a hit. Word spread, and we started making a hundred cookies each night, instead of seventy-five.

The free-lunch chocolate chips also worked out the way we planned, because the winner never came back alone, so we sold two or three extra lunches when we gave away one for free.

Then an unexpected situation arose. A few days after the start of the contest, eight people found chocolate chips in their sandwiches. The first two winners were mothers; we gave them their certificates gladly. Next was Dao's baby-sitter friend, Kathy. She was thrilled. A five-year-old nearly ate his chocolate chip, but his older brother, who understood the contest, rescued it and claimed the prize. And the last winner was a girl from out of town. We were glad she won, because we hoped she'd tell her friends back home about us.

Then just before one o'clock two girls and a boy who lived around the block came up to us at the card table with chocolate chips pressed into the fillings of their tuna sandwiches. Gina gave them a suspicious look.

"Something's wrong here," she said. "We only put in five chips a day."

"Well we've got three of them," said one of the girls, a lanky fifth-grader with braces on her teeth.

"But we've already had five turned in," Gina argued. "This makes eight, so these must be fakes."

"Mine's a real chocolate chip," said the little boy.

"Mine's real, too," said the other girl.

Buck came over to take a look. It was he, after all, who had put the chips in the sandwiches this morning. "I never put three chips in the same kind of sandwich," Buck informed them. "I always spread them around."

"You must have messed up today," the girl with the braces told him. "You owe us three free lunches."

Most of the customers had stopped what they were doing to see what was going on. Lizzie and I joined them. "You brought in your own chips," Lizzie accused the three kids.

"Prove it," the girl with the braces said.

Lizzie glared at her. Of course we couldn't prove it. A chocolate chip was a chocolate chip. There was a tense moment of silence, when no one would give in.

"Look," I snarled, taking a step closer to the three. "You know you planted those chocolate chips in the sandwiches. Just admit it."

"No, we didn't," said the girl. She had small, hungry-looking eyes and a mean mouth.

But Lizzie had another idea. Casually she shrugged, glanced at the audience that was watching to see who would win this battle of the free lunches, and said, "Go ahead, Gina. Let them have free lunches tomorrow. Today is the last day with the chips anyway. We've got that other contest slated for tomorrow, remember?"

Gina, Buck, and I all nodded as if we really knew what she was talking about. We knew Lizzie was up to something, and it seemed wisest to play along with her. "Besides," she added, "our food must be pretty good if some people would go to these lengths to eat more of it."

A couple of people smiled, and the tension broke as Gina handed over the certificates. The four of us nodded to each other and went back to work, and our three devious customers went off with their undeserved prizes.

Later, cleaning up, Lizzie explained to us what she'd done. "The customer is always right," she said. "Not that they were right, but we were stupid to pick something like a chocolate chip that's so easy to get a hold of. From now on, maybe I can make a special mark on five of the bags. That way there's no way anyone can know ahead of time what they'll need to win."

"Much better," Buck said.

Gina and I agreed, and then Gina said proudly, "You see? There's nothing we can't handle. We can overcome all odds and still make a profit."

The Adidas box now held over fifty dollars. But it held something else, too. On the bottom lay the note recording Victoria Chubb's charge for one lunch. And I had the sinking feeling she'd be back to pay it.

8

Victoria Chubb paid us back, all right. The day she did began like any other day that summer. It was eleven-fifteen the following Wednesday, and two customers were already outside, waiting for the squeak of the garage door to signal our opening. By twelve we were in full swing. Lizzie's idea of putting a special mark on the sandwich bags worked out beautifully. Each day her design changed, from a fluorescent yellow sun to a shocking pink flower or a glowing green tree. Cheating was now impossible, and the three chocolate chip cheaters had not returned to redeem their coupons for lunch the following day. Good riddance to them.

Victoria Chubb could not have arrived at a worse time. A little kid had just spilled half his carton of juice on the garage floor, and Gina and Buck were inside getting a sponge and towels to clean it up, when Lizzie spotted her.

“Look who’s back,” she whispered, her blue eyes narrowing. “And not alone, either.” Two people were getting out of a small red Toyota at the end of my driveway.

I looked up from the cash box, where I was making change, and saw Victoria Chubb coming up the driveway with a man who could have been her big brother. The guy didn’t look that much older than Tommy. From his tight curly hair that nearly matched hers in color, I knew they were related. And by the smug look on her face I knew she was up to something. So what, I thought, as they came closer. Even if he is a restaurant inspector, why should we care? We haven’t done anything wrong. Little did I realize how mistaken I was.

“Hi, Roger,” Victoria said. “I’m back to pay you the dollar I owe you. And to introduce you to my uncle, Mr. Chubb. He works for the County Health Department,” she added in an unnecessarily loud voice.

“I’m Phil Chubb,” Victoria’s uncle said, extending his hand to me. His smile was friendly, and the way he was dressed did not look official at all. He didn’t even have on a suit, but instead wore gray pants and a red-and-white-striped shirt.

“Nice to meet you,” I said, wiping my palm

against my jeans before I took his.

"I take it you people have a permit to operate a food service," Phil Chubb said, sounding casual yet official at the same time.

Luckily, before I could answer, two eight-year-old girls burst in front of Victoria and her uncle. "I want a heart-shaped peanut butter and jelly," one demanded. "And a grape juice and a cookie."

"Me, too!" cried the other. "Only I want a spade and my mom does, too. She's in the car waiting for us. We're going to have a picnic at the park."

I smiled politely at Victoria and Phil, then turned to Lizzie. Her eyes caught mine and grew big, as if to say, "What in the world are we going to do?" But I just said coolly, "Two spades and one heart peanut butter and jelly, Lizzie. I'll get the juice and cookies."

As I started toward the refrigerator I saw Phil looking around curiously. He glanced at the spilled juice just as Buck and Gina appeared with my mother's kitchen sponge and some old cleaning rags to clean it up. I felt his eye on me as I opened the refrigerator.

When I got back to the table, Lizzie had the bags ready to go.

"Would you like to order?" I asked Victoria and her uncle, trying to sound as businesslike as possible.

"I'll have a tuna diamond, apple juice, and a cookie," Victoria said. "I've got the dollar I owe you. And I see your prices have gone up," she noted as Gina and Buck returned to their stations.

"Yep," Buck said, not looking her in the eye. "A dollar twenty-five. What would you like?" he asked Victoria's uncle.

"Nothing, thanks," he said. For a second Phil looked a little embarrassed. Then he said, "I meant it about the permit. It's my job to be sure all eating establishments have one before they serve food to the public. I'm not here to hassle you. But it is the law." He pulled out his wallet and took out a card, which he handed to me. It read: PHILLIP CHUBB: PUBLIC HEALTH SANITARIAN. It gave his office phone number and address, too.

"So, how do we get a permit?" Lizzie asked, walking over to examine the card more closely. It definitely had a more authentic look than the one Victoria had given us. "We'll just get one, that's all," she said confidently.

"They cost money," Victoria said. "And first you have to hand in your layout. And a menu. Before they'll even consider you for a permit." Her uncle nodded.

"And this place has violations, doesn't it?" Victoria went on enthusiastically. "Your refrigerator has to be a certain temperature, right Uncle Phil?"

"Below forty-five degrees to store cold foods," he said. "Is your refrigerator below forty-five?" Phil asked me.

"I don't know," I said.

"You need hair restraints. Isn't that what they call them?" Victoria said.

"Hair nets for long hair like yours," her uncle said, nodding at Lizzie's long silky mane. "And hats for the guys and girls with shorter hair." I saw Gina grimace. Knowing how she felt about style, I was sure she wouldn't want to have to wear a hat like Buck and me.

"And a sign in the bathroom telling employees to wash their hands," Victoria added. "And a choking poster the customers can see. And paper towels and soap in the bathroom at all times." Victoria ticked off our violations like she was reciting the Pledge of Allegiance.

"Did you wash those apples before you passed them out?" Phil asked.

"No," I admitted. "We just polished them a little."

"They have to be washed," he told me. Then he pulled a sheet of paper out of his shirt pocket. "Also your wiping cloths have to be used only for wiping up spills. You can't just pull something out of the kitchen like you did. I'm afraid I'll have to write you up," he said. But he truly sounded sorry. "You kids have a great idea here. But you're going to have to abide by the rules. And the first rule is you must have a permit."

"We'll get one," I promised.

Several customers were coming up the driveway, and I didn't want Victoria and her uncle blocking the counter. "And I'll wash those apples right away."

"You need the *permit* right away," Phil said. Again he sounded regretful. But firm. "I'm afraid I have to close you down for today. You see, now that I've been here, if anything were to go wrong or somebody got sick — not that I think they would, but if they did — I could lose my job for allowing you to operate without a permit."

"You mean . . ." I began.

"Close us down!" Buck bellowed.

"He means you are in violation right this minute," Victoria answered triumphantly. "Until you get a permit you're out of business!"

Her uncle gave her a wary look as he shook his head. My stomach took a sick dive. "I'm afraid she's right," Phil said.

"Please, just let us serve the people who are

here," Lizzie begged. Lizzie, always so calm and confident, sounded truly upset. "Then we'll do whatever you ask."

"Well . . . OK. But first, wash those apples," Phil directed me. "Finish up with the people who are waiting. Then put up a CLOSED sign and shut the door. I'll sit down with you and we can go over what you'll need."

Buck looked ready to cry as he went to get the CLOSED sign — almost an hour before closing. I felt ready to cry, Gina squeezed back a tear, and Lizzie gave Victoria a look that would have withered a plastic flower. But Victoria was too busy enjoying her lunch — and her victory — to notice. However, I caught Lizzie's eye and let her know that I completely agreed with her. Victoria Chubb was a much nastier person than we could ever have imagined.

It was truly hard to believe that Phil Chubb was in any way related to Victoria. After we had closed Aces for the day and put away all the perishables in the refrigerator, which Phil tested and found to be forty-three degrees, the six of us sat around the picnic table and went over what we'd need to get back into business. There were six of us because no one had the nerve to tell Victoria to get lost. And she loved sitting there beside her uncle, adding her opinion whenever she found an opportunity.

"Let's see," Phil said. "To get the permit you'll need to submit a floor plan and menu to our office. That shouldn't be too hard."

Gina took a sheet of paper from my notebook and started to copy down the menu. Buck, who was good at sketching, began to draw the inside of my garage. "Just label the counter, the refrigerator, and the seating space," Phil directed. "It doesn't have to be elaborate."

"Did you tell them how much they have to pay for the permit?" Victoria asked.

"I'm getting to that," Phil said. The way he said it, I could tell he'd had just about enough of her comments.

"We charge for our permits by seating capacity," Phil explained. "The cheapest one, which you'd qualify for, is twenty dollars. It's a seasonal permit for an establishment seating fewer than fifteen people."

"We really don't seat anybody," Gina pointed out.

"Which is to your benefit," Phil replied. "If you seated twenty or more people, you'd have to provide toilet facilities for customers instead of just employees."

“My mother would never allow strangers going into her bathroom,” I said, as Buck handed Phil his sketch.

“This looks fine,” he told him. “For seasonal permits we’re not too fussy. But before you opened up you should have had this layout, a menu, your application, and the fee into our office.”

“You’re supposed to do it twenty-one days in advance,” Victoria said smugly. “So you’ll just have to wait twenty-one days to get the permit.”

“Twenty-one days!” Gina and I said in unison. Lizzie groaned, and we all looked desperately at Phil. Twenty-one days out of business and the summer would be just about over.

“We didn’t know that,” Gina said. “Honest, we didn’t.”

“No one knew,” I chimed in. “Believe me, if my parents knew they would have told me. They would never have let me do anything illegal in their garage.”

“I’m sure you didn’t realize it,” Phil said.

“I told them,” Victoria said.

Phil ignored her. “I think I may be able to help you out some,” he said. “We’re not too busy this time of year. Most of the seasonal permits are issued in April. How long do you think it would take you to get all the things you need to come up to standard?"

I began making a mental list. We'd need the choking and hand-washing signs, which Phil told us his office would provide. We'd have to get hairnets, make hats, wash the fruit, and get paper towels for the bathroom. There wasn't really anything too difficult.

"I think we could do it overnight," I said, looking directly at Victoria. "Of course I'd have to explain the hand-washing signs and the paper towels in the bathroom to my parents. But other than that, I don't see any problem."

"Do you have twenty dollars?" Victoria asked.

"Yes," I told her sharply. "In fact, we have enough for several permits."

"You only need one," Phil said. "I agree, with a little work you can easily come up to standard. This is a pretty basic operation. Let's see, if you'll fill out this application, and I can get down to the office by three and hand in your menu and the floor plan, I bet Marie could type me up a permit and have it ready by five."

"You mean today!" Lizzie exclaimed. "We could get it today? And reopen tomorrow?"

"I don't see why not," Phil said with a grin. When Phil smiled his eyes crinkled up, and I decided — in spite of his last name being the same as Victoria's — that I actually liked him. "As I told you, things are slow, especially with seasonal permits. Nothing you're doing is going to cause any public sickness as far as I can see. And we're not out to close up restaurants. We wouldn't have a job if we did that."

"But if you get complaints . . ." Victoria began.

"We've only had one complaint," her uncle said, looking her squarely in the eye. "It was a valid one. A restaurant operating without a permit. But I've now made a preliminary inspection and except for the permit, which the establishment will have by this evening, I see no reason to shut down this business."

Victoria glared at her uncle. His tone to her was not friendly. We all avoided looking at her, and instead started thanking Phil. Suddenly Victoria stood up and headed off to the car without saying good-bye. As she stormed off, her usual confident walk was an angry stomp. Phil just shrugged, and a few minutes later he followed her with our menu, floor plan, permit application, and twenty dollars. As the small red car took off we looked at each other with satisfied smiles.

"Eat your heart out, Victoria Chubb," I said.

"And eat it out right here," Lizzie added. "Because we're going to get our permit and keep going. And there's nothing you can do to stop us."

But that, as we would soon see, wasn't exactly true. We hadn't seen the last of Victoria Chubb yet.

9

Phil Chubb was better than his word. At five-thirty that same afternoon he was back. From my bedroom window I saw his little red car pull into the driveway. Right behind it I saw my mother's car pull in. I tore downstairs and outside. To have my mother greeted by a restaurant inspector before I could explain things might prove dangerous.

"Hi, Phil," I said. "This is my mother. Mom, this is Phil Chubb, Victoria's uncle. He's been giving us some help with the luncheonette."

My mother smiled as she and Phil shook hands. "I'm Joan Gordon," she said. "What kind of help have you been giving Roger?"

"Phil's a restaurant inspector," I explained.

My mother gulped. I'm sure she thought he'd already gone over the entire kitchen and discovered that she never cleaned behind the refrigerator or the stove. "Did we pass?" she asked with a grimace.

"I'm merely inspecting the business operation," Phil explained. "They have a few things to work on. But overall, it's a pretty sound job." My mother looked relieved as Phil went on. "Your permit is all set," he said handing me a manila envelope. "It should be displayed where customers can see it. I'm also giving you the hand-washing and choking posters. Be sure to get them up, too."

"Thanks," I said. "We really had no idea what was involved. And if it weren't for Victoria sticking her nose in where — " I quickly caught myself. My mother was frowning, and I had to remember I was talking to Victoria's uncle.

"Victoria can be pesty," Phil said. "But she means well. She's got her own set of problems. And sometimes people don't give her a chance."

"So, we can reopen tomorrow?" I asked. I wanted to change the subject. Victoria Chubb had acted like a bratty rich kid, and I wasn't about to start feeling sorry for her.

"Business as usual," Phil assured me, heading toward his car. "And I'll be dropping by again someday soon to make sure you've corrected all the violations."

"No problem," I said as he got into his car.

"What violations?" my mother asked. But she was looking at me curiously, and suddenly I felt grown-up. My mother loved to talk about her real estate business, and I realized I would enjoy talking to her about my business, too.

"Nothing major," I said. "But did you know that the refrigerator has to be forty-five degrees or colder to keep cold foods? Ours is forty-three. And did you know that you have to wash fruit before you can sell it? And wiping cloths have to be used only for. . . ."

With our permit framed and hung next to our first dollar, our choking poster up, and all of our violations corrected, we were ready to sail through the rest of the summer without a snag. Lizzie had done some more profit predictions, and the way she figured it, if business went on as it was, four hundred dollars by the end of the summer was a low figure. We could top seven hundred.

She made this prediction on a Friday. The following Tuesday she revised it. "We may not hit three hundred at this rate," she announced glumly. The day, hot and sticky with a glaring bright sun, had been a business disaster for us.

"Where *is* everybody?" Buck lamented at twelve forty-five. He was on his third baloney sandwich, which he'd downed with three cartons of grape drink. "I don't want to dehydrate in this heat," he told us.

"At the pool," Gina said. "Where I'm going the minute we close. My mother bought me this gorgeous new bathing suit, which I can't wait to wear. It's too hot to do anything but swim today anyway. Can we close early?"

"Not yet. There's still one more customer coming," Lizzie said. I knew without looking, by her unenthusiastic tone, who that customer was.

Victoria came to a smooth stop and hopped off her bike. She had on red shorts, a red-and-white-striped halter top, and red-framed sunglasses. Her curly hair was pulled away from her face by two shiny red combs. In spite of the heat she looked cool.

"What a great outfit," Gina said under her breath.

"I've just been to the pool," Victoria announced. "Mobbed. Positively wall-to-wall people. Everyone's over there." She looked around the empty garage pointedly, as if to remind us they were not there.

"What do you want for lunch?" Gina said impatiently. "We're just about to close."

"Let me try a tuna spade and an orange drink," Victoria said. "I just had a hamburger at the pool.

It was terrible. Thin and greasy. And the roll wasn't fresh. Your food is a lot better."

I glanced suspiciously at Victoria. Something told me she was setting us up.

But Buck actually smiled at her. "Thanks, Victoria," he said, adding a little extra tuna to the sandwich before cutting it into a spade. "Maybe we should put in a pool here," he said, giving me a wink.

"Yeah," I said, with a smirk, imagining what my parents would say.

"If you can't bring a pool to the luncheonette, why not bring the luncheonette to the pool?" Victoria asked.

"What do you mean?" Buck asked slowly. Gina, Lizzie, and I turned our attention to Victoria. She was on to something, all right. That smug, triumphant look was already starting to steal across her face again.

"It could be done," she said. "In fact, I've just come from a little talk with the pool director."

"And?" Gina asked.

"Oh, I just mentioned the possibility of a bag-lunch business. Orders would be taken in advance, and the lunches would be delivered to people at the pool."

Buck's eyes were getting that excited gleam I'd seen several times before this summer, when an idea came along that he liked. "Well, what did the director say?"

"He saw no problem with it. People can bring in their own lunches now. This is really a variation on that. When the lunches arrived at the pool I'd ring a bell, and everyone who'd ordered one from me could come to pick it up."

"*You'd* ring a bell?" I asked. "They'd pick it up from *you*?"

"Come on," Victoria said. And suddenly her voice had a softer tone. "You know it's a great idea. And you know you need it. Why don't you let me do it? I'll take charge of taking all the orders and making the deliveries. All you guys have to do is supply the lunches."

The four of us looked at each other. It did sound like a way to boost business. And we would need someone else to handle it. It took the four of us to prepare the food and handle things at Aces. But Victoria Chubb was the last person on earth I wanted working with us.

"I'm calling a meeting for one o'clock," I said abruptly.

Gina made a face. "I want to go swimming," she complained. "My bathing suit will be out of style by the time I get to the pool."

"This will be short," I promised. "We'll vote on this new suggestion of Victoria's." I turned to

Victoria. "We have to vote, so we'll let you know later."

"When?" Victoria pressed.

"Come back at two," I told her.

Victoria grinned confidently as she took her lunch bag and hopped on her bike. "See you at two," she called, disappearing down the driveway.

"Let's make this fast," Gina said, as we all assembled in my room. The tips of her short blonde bangs were damp with sweat, and Buck was already starting to take off his shirt. The small fan I put on at night was about as good as a dog wagging his tail when it came to cooling down the room. "I say we let Victoria do it," Gina voted.

"Me, too," Buck said. "I've got some ideas for advertising that will blow you away. I just hope we can put up signs at the pool."

Lizzie and I looked at them warily. "I'm not sure I want to let her do it," I said. "I don't trust her. She just wants to get in on this with us. And she'll probably try to take over."

"I agree with Roger," Lizzie said. "Look at how she's been so far, trying to force her way in, then turning us in to her uncle."

"She doesn't have to become a partner," Buck argued. "She'll be working *for* us, that's all."

"Besides," Gina said, "she's going to camp at

the end of August. Let her do it for a while. If it works out, when she goes to camp we can hire someone else. She'll be so rich when she gets back she won't want to be delivering sandwiches for anybody."

"We'll have to pay her," I said. "Can you imagine how much she'll want to be paid? And there go our profits."

"Not if we add on a delivery charge," Gina pointed out. "We charge the same price plus a delivery charge, which goes to Victoria."

I considered this. If Victoria would go for it, maybe having her deliver the lunches could work out. She would really just be buying them from us, then pedalling off to deliver them. We'd hardly ever see her. And we sure could sell a lot more.

Lizzie was beginning to look thoughtful, too. "We've got to do something," she conceded. "Business is not very good. And if we wait, the summer will be over."

I remember how Phil had said Victoria had her own problems, and how people didn't give her a chance. "Maybe we could try it," I said. "On a temporary basis. We'll give her a week, and if it works we'll keep her on."

Gina stood up with relief. "Everyone agrees, right?" she said. We all nodded. "Then I'm off to the pool. Suntan, here I come!"

"I'm right behind you," Lizzie said.

"Me, too!" Buck added.

"I'll be over later," I said glumly. "After I share the good news with Victoria."

But even as I said it, I couldn't fully believe it was as good as it sounded.

Victoria was back promptly at two. I met her in the driveway. I had on my swim trunks, with a towel draped around my neck. I wanted to make it clear to her that this was a quick business discussion and that I had other things to do.

"So?" she asked eagerly.

"So it's okay as long as you don't cause any problems," I said, unable to keep from sounding irritated.

"Problems?" Victoria asked incredulously, her brown eyes wide.

"You know what I mean," I said. "I haven't got time to go into it now. And you're not a partner. You're working for us."

For a second Victoria looked hurt. So I quickly continued. "That might change someday. But for now, we're giving this project a week. And lunches still cost a dollar twenty-five. You can add on a delivery charge — "

"Twenty-five cents," Victoria interrupted.

"And that's your salary," I told her.

Victoria grinned. "Then I've made two-fifty already," she said. With that she pulled a thick roll of bills and a pack of small papers from her red shorts pocket. "My orders for tomorrow," she explained. "All paid in advance. After I cleared it with the director of the pool I did an informal survey of the pool today and found a lot of interest in a hand-delivered lunch. These kids paid me in advance. There are others who were going to, but they didn't have the cash with them."

She handed me the packet of slips. Sure enough, each kid's name, sandwich type and shape, beverage, and dessert choice were neatly checked off. In spite of my basic dislike for Victoria, I couldn't help but be impressed. Right here we had ten guaranteed sales. For tomorrow! And there were more kids interested.

"This is pretty good," I admitted. "But what would you have done if we hadn't voted you in on this?" I asked, unwilling to give Victoria too much praise at once.

"I would have done the same thing," she told me briskly. "I just would have bought ten lunches from you for a dollar twenty-five and delivered them for a dollar fifty. Actually, I probably could have made them cheaper at home myself. It's really only a professional courtesy to you that I'm telling you what I'm doing in the first place."

I felt a churn of anger begin in the pit of my stomach. Professional courtesy, my eye! Victoria Chubb was so jealous of our idea, she would do anything to be part of it. Right then I wanted to tell her to forget the whole thing and never set foot on my property again. The nerve of her, taking all those orders in advance.

But better judgment stopped me. The thought of ten sales already firm for tomorrow, along with the realization that all of us had voted her in — so we'd all have to vote her out — stopped me.

But I wasn't going to let her off that easy. "Look, Victoria," I said. "If you're going to work for us, you've got to do a little more than just deliver sandwiches."

"Like what?" she asked.

"There's a lot that goes on behind the scenes in this business. Like shopping, for instance. Right now I'm headed to join the partners at the pool. After all, we've worked all day. Tonight Buck and Lizzie will be baking more cookies. And Gina and I have some other work to do. It would really make a difference if we had someone to shop for us this afternoon."

At first Victoria didn't look too interested.

"It's part of the responsibility that goes along with maybe eventually becoming a partner," I said. I had noticed that something about the word *partner* seemed to interest Victoria. "And," I reminded her, "it would be a real shame if we didn't have the supplies we needed to fill your orders tomorrow."

"Sure," Victoria said, a little uncertainly. "What do we need?"

I started rattling off a list. "Six cans of tuna, three loaves of bread, four twelve-packs of juice, and a large jar of grape jelly. That should cover it."

"No problem," Victoria said. "I'll pay for it with my own money, save the receipt, and you can pay me back later."

"Good," I said, starting down the driveway toward the pool. "Drop it off any time after six tonight," I told her.

"Sure thing," Victoria called happily as she got on her bike. "See you later."

"Yeah," I said as she disappeared around the corner. Puzzled, I headed toward the pool. Because even though Victoria Chubb was coming in a little clearer, I still couldn't figure her out completely.

Although it was hard to admit, Victoria's delivery services marked the start of our days of big profits. Some days she delivered as many as twenty-five lunches. The first week she worked for us she did it alone. She'd make two or three runs with the big metal basket on the back of her bike filled with lunch bags. Then she'd blow this huge silver whistle she wore around her neck like a gym teacher, and all the kids who'd ordered lunch from her would come running. After about a week however, some of her customers at the pool started getting mad if they weren't served on the first run. They didn't like watching their friends eat while they had to sit and wait for Victoria to return with her second — and sometimes third — batch of lunches. So Victoria hired an assistant.

His name was Bart Kelly, and he was a fifth-grader with a mouthful of silver braces, and black-framed dark glasses that he never took off. He was new to the neighborhood when Victoria discovered him.

"Can that kid Bart talk?" Buck asked one day when Bart had been working for Victoria just over a week, and we were in my room talking about menu changes. There'd been several requests for marshmallow fluff, and we needed to vote whether or not to make an addition to our sandwich list.

"He can say 'I'm here to get the deliveries,' " Gina answered. "But nothing else."

"He's weird," Lizzie said. We all agreed, for Bart had never smiled, nodded, or uttered a word to any of us except for the shortest remark he could manage when picking up the lunches.

"And he never takes off those glasses," Lizzie went on. "And they're so dark you can't see his eyes. I wonder if he even has eyes."

"Maybe he's an alien," Buck said. "Maybe he's been programmed by extraterrestrial beings to ask for sandwiches and nothing else."

"Yeah," Gina said. "And he's probably been sent here from a far-off planet to find the Secret of Human Sandwich Making."

"Very possible," Buck agreed. "The kid is definitely strange."

"He may be strange," I said. "But look at this." I brought out the Adidas box and held up a thick wad of bills. "With Victoria and Bart guaranteeing us sales of twenty dollars a day, we're using what we make downstairs for shopping. Their money is pure profit."

"So we're making twenty a day?" Lizzie asked.

"About that," I said.

"And there are only three more weeks until Labor Day," she calculated. "Fifteen days at twenty dollars a day. We'll be well over eight hundred for the summer."

"I vote we spend some of it on a party," Gina said. "A farewell party. For us and anyone we want to invite."

"Yes," Lizzie agreed. "We can invite our best customers, our parents, and — "

"I've got a better idea," Buck interrupted. "You know how we had a Grand Opening. How about a Grand Closing? I bet it would be the first one in the history of business!"

"I do like that better," Lizzie agreed. "And we can still invite the people we especially want to come."

"A Grand Closing," Gina murmured. "It has a nice sound to it. But aren't we here to vote on fluff? I want to get to the pool."

"That's right," Lizzie conceded. "We can discuss that later. Right now the issue is that two kids have asked me, and Victoria said she got three requests for peanut butter and fluff at the pool. One was for jelly and fluff."

"Jelly and fluff is a dentist's delight," Buck said. "Guaranteed to make cavities, whether you want them or not."

"Not if you brush your teeth right after eating it," Lizzie said.

"How many kids do you see brushing at the pool?" Buck asked.

"The question is: do we add fluff to the menu?" I said impatiently.

"It would mean changing the signs," Gina said. "And there's something so babyish about peanut butter and fluff. I think it would make our menu seem junky."

For a second we all considered this. I knew what she meant — so far we'd kept the idea good for younger kids, but with an appeal to the older ones, too. Peanut butter and fluff could turn people off — especially parents.

"I vote no," Gina said.

"I guess I agree," Buck said.

"Ditto," I said.

"Me, too," Lizzie concluded for us. "And if anyone asks, we'll just tell them we may consider it for next year. But for now the menu is set."

"Settled," Buck said, getting up. "I'm on my way over to the pool. Anybody going over?"

"I am," I said.

"Wait till you see the new *Teenstyle* magazine," Gina said to Lizzie. "I just got it yesterday. All the fall clothes are in it. I'll bring it and meet you by the drinking fountain in an hour."

We all got up, and as I got ready to go I couldn't help but think about how great things were going. Not only had the weather the past week been super — hot, dry, and sunny — but business had been super, too. And as I quickly changed and grabbed my towel I had no reason to think the sun wouldn't keep right on shining on Aces throughout the entire summer.

10

Our darkest day actually *was* a dark day. Occurring just a week later, it was gray and gloomy. The TV had predicted this weather and Victoria had only taken three orders for sandwiches. She'd given the slips to Bart, who delivered them to me with the words "For tomorrow."

On Saturday Victoria was leaving for her week at investment camp. But she assured us Bart would be able to handle the entire delivery business while she was away. "I told him he can get someone to help out if it gets to be too much work," she told me that Friday. "Only until I get back, of course."

She had followed me, without invitation, to my room, while the partners were downstairs cleaning up. She had plunked herself down on the edge of my bed and was explaining to me the arrangements she'd made for her absence.

"Bart knows what I expect," she said, sounding

like a teacher. "But still, you'd better keep an eye on him. He can be a little strange at times."

"Does he talk to you?" I asked, taking the Adidas box from my closet to get the money we'd need for our late afternoon shopping.

"He's quiet," Victoria said. "Of course, I interviewed him before I hired him," she added. "And he talked during the interview."

Interview! Kids who knew Victoria would never have considered working for her — much less being interviewed by her. But Bart was new to this area. She was lucky he didn't know any better.

I lifted the cover of the Adidas box. "Wow!" Victoria said. "What's all that?"

"Our profits," I said. "We'll probably be up to around seven or eight hundred by the end of the season," I said, exaggerating slightly. "Seven hundred dollars to be divided up among the partners."

I knew I was being a little mean to Victoria. But I felt she deserved it. She certainly had done all she could to ruin us. And now she was heading off to investment camp with five hundred dollars her parents had *given* her. It didn't seem fair.

"At investment camp your seven hundred dollars could turn into a thousand," Victoria said. "If you knew how to manage them. Do you know anything about the stock market, Roger?" she challenged.

"I know it can crash," I said, suddenly more annoyed than ever with Victoria. I hadn't invited her into my room, and I wasn't in the mood to discuss the stock market, which, to be perfectly honest, I didn't understand at all.

"For your information, although the market does go up and down, and although it may occasionally drop to record lows, it is highly unlikely the market will ever crash again like it did when our grandparents were young," Victoria told me in that know-it-all tone she hadn't used since she told her uncle about our violations. "Special rules have been made to be sure that doesn't happen again. Besides, the wise investor doesn't put all his or her money into one stock."

"Big deal," I said.

"From what my father tells me," Victoria went on, "timing is critical if you play the market. Take now, for instance. This summer — "

"Take now," I interrupted her, "and it's time to leave." I abruptly cut her off. I wasn't in the mood for a lesson on stocks and bonds from Victoria Chubb. I stood up and put the shoe box in the closet. "Good luck at camp," I told her, folding two tens into my pocket. "Now I have to go shopping for a couple of things we need for lunch tomorrow."

I marched downstairs with Victoria behind me. The last I saw of her she was pedaling down the street. In some ways, I thought to myself, it was a relief to know I wouldn't have to see her again for a week.

Later, trying to remember how the disaster could have occurred, I went over the next few days carefully. It wasn't hard. On Friday afternoon I did the shopping alone. Buck was going to his grandparents' for the weekend, Lizzie had a dentist appointment, and Gina's father had promised to take her shopping.

"For clothes," she told me when I suggested they could pick up the few groceries we needed. "Not for food."

So I headed to the Grand Union alone. We only needed juice, a jar of peanut butter, two loaves of bread, and a few cans of tuna fish. In the cookie aisle, who should I spot but Bart? He had a small red shopping basket hooked over his arm, and he was staring intently at the large bag of caramel crunch cookies he held in one hand and a bag of chocolate mint bars in the other.

"I'd get the mint bars," I said, coming up behind

him. "My mother says those caramel crunch cookies will yank the fillings right out of your teeth."

Bart jumped. He gave me a funny half smile. I glanced in the shopping basket. Three bags of candy, a box of doughnuts and several bags of candy bars were already in it.

"Looks like someone has a sweet tooth," I said, trying to make conversation.

"Yeah," Bart said.

From behind his dark glasses I could barely see his eyes, but I thought they were wide with surprise. For a moment we just stood there in the cookie aisle, neither of us saying anything.

"Have a nice weekend," I finally said.

"Yeah," Bart said as I walked down the aisle.

Saturday and Sunday were quiet days. Saturday my dad took me to the driving range to hit golf balls. Sunday we had a cookout at home. Tommy's girlfriend, Cindy, had invited him to spend the weekend at her family's camp, so it was just the three of us. For a change, my parents didn't bug me much, even though right in the middle of barbecuing the chicken my mother said sadly, "I do miss Tommy. And he hasn't even gone away to college yet. Although," she added, "I won't miss Cindy calling here a dozen times a day."

On Monday the four of us were back at work as usual. We were set up and running by eleven-thirty. Bart brought in fifteen orders and made two runs to deliver them. We closed at one as usual, cleaned up, and headed to my room to make the grocery list and count the money. I went to get the Adidas box from the closet, and my first hint of something not being quite right was how light it felt as I lifted it from the shelf. I knew then what I'd find when I opened it. And I found just what I expected. The box was cleaned out — empty!

"No!" I cried in disbelief. Buck, Gina, and Lizzie looked at me. "We've been robbed!" I shouted.

Everyone rushed over as I held out the empty box. "There was over five hundred dollars in here on Friday," I cried. "It's gone!"

"It can't be gone!" Gina yelled. She ran to the closet and started poking around on the floor. "Maybe it dropped out," she said.

"It didn't drop out," I cried back. "I haven't opened the box since Friday."

"Now keep calm, everyone," Lizzie ordered. "Roger, think. When was the last time you actually saw the money in the box?"

"Friday after lunch," I said. "Victoria was here with me. She was talking about going to camp, and I . . ."

"Maybe she took it," Gina said.

"Victoria?" I questioned. "She couldn't have

taken it. She left the room when I did. I saw her ride away on her bike. Besides, she's so rich she doesn't need any more money."

"Well, I didn't take it," Buck said. "And I *need* money."

"Me, too," Gina said.

"Just a second," Lizzie interrupted. "Did you move the money? Put it somewhere else and maybe forget?"

"No, I absolutely did not," I said.

"Then it must be what the police would call an inside job," Lizzie concluded.

"What do you mean by that?" I asked quickly. Did anyone actually think *I* could have taken the money? Or my parents? Or Tommy?

"Whoever took it had to be able to get into your room easily, Roger," Lizzie pointed out.

Buck jumped up and ran to my window. "No one got in through the window," he reported, showing us the tightly closed screen.

"The door doesn't look as if it's been forced open either," Gina said.

"I never lock it," I retorted.

"I think we should call the police," Lizzie said.

"Just a second," I said. I knew if we were going to call the police we'd have to call my parents first. I couldn't very well have a patrol car pulling up outside with all the neighbors wondering what was going on, and not let my parents know about it.

"Let's think this over first," I said. "Who has a motive?" I'd seen on television that there had to be a motive when a crime was committed.

"Everyone," Buck said. "Doesn't everyone want more money?"

"Everyone except Victoria Chubb. She already has more money than she knows what to do with," Lizzie pointed out. "Besides, how could she get into your room?" She paused a second. "Do you think Tommy could have borrowed it?"

"Tommy!" I cried. Even though she'd said "borrowed it," I couldn't believe anyone would think Tommy would touch our money. "My brother would never take anything — especially money — from my room," I said angrily. Then I remembered Bart. I'd seen him at the grocery store, and he had seemed uncomfortable about meeting me. "You know, I saw Bart," I said. "And he was acting a little weird."

"He always acts a little weird," Gina said.

"Yes, but he was spending quite a lot of money," I said. "On candy. I think we should try to find him."

"How could he have gotten into your room?" Lizzie asked.

"During lunch today he could have slipped in,"

I said. "Remember, it was pretty busy here today. And I haven't looked at the money since Friday. Victoria may have told him where we kept it, and he could have just walked in when we weren't looking."

"What's his last name?" Lizzie asked. "We can call the operator and see if he's listed. We'll go right to his house and catch him off guard."

"Kelly," Buck said. "Bart Kelly. Does anyone know what street he lives on?"

No one knew, and when I called information and asked for Bart Kelly the operator said I had to know one of his parents' first names or his street before she could find him out of the nearly two hundred Kellys listed.

"If Bart took the money, he's sure done a great job of covering his tracks. With Victoria out of town there's no way we'll find him soon," Gina said.

Buck groaned. "Isn't there something we can do?"

For a second we all just stared at the blue rug and my bedroom floor. "We can call the police," Lizzie finally said again.

Although I didn't want to do it I couldn't stand the thought of sitting there doing nothing. "Let me talk to Tommy first," I said. Even though Tommy wasn't supposed to be woken up, this seemed enough of an emergency to make him lose a few minutes of sleep.

Quickly I went to my brother's door. I knocked softly. No answer. I knocked a little louder. I heard the springs creak but no voice telling me to come in. Finally I pounded on the door.

From inside came a muffled "Huh?"

I opened the door. The room was dark and cool as night. Tommy had put beach towels over the shades, and he'd bought an old air conditioner at a garage sale, which rattled loudly as it blew cool air.

"Tommy?" I whispered. "I have to ask you something. It's important."

"Wha. . . ?" Tommy said, half sitting up.

"We've been robbed," I said. "All the money I keep in the Adidas box is gone. Should I call the police?"

Tommy groped for the light beside his bed, turned it on, and squinted at me as the brightness filled his room. "You were robbed?"

"Our money's gone," I said. "Personally, I think Victoria Chubb took it. But some of the kids think it was Bart." I didn't mention that he, too, had been named as a suspect. "It could have been anybody, I guess, but . . ."

"So why do you have to call the police?" Tommy asked. He was starting to wake up but the whole situation still wasn't completely clear to him.

"It was over five hundred dollars, that's why," I said impatiently. "No one knows Bart's address. Victoria Chubb is off at camp. . . ."

"Oh yeah, Victoria," Tommy said. "She left you a note."

"A note?" I asked. "When?"

"Friday. I was coming out of the bathroom, and she came out of your room and said she'd left something there and — "

"She was in the house and *I* wasn't here?" I yelled.

"Yes. She came out of your room and gave me a note. I didn't see you all weekend," Tommy said apologetically. "And I didn't know if you'd want Mom or Dad to read it, seeing it was from a girl. So I didn't give it to them. And then I forgot about it. Until now. . . ."

"So where is it?"

"In my top drawer," Tommy said.

I raced over and yanked open Tommy's dresser. There on the top of a mound of mismatched socks was a neatly folded sheet of lined paper. I opened it and read:

Dear Aces Partners:

I have taken your summer profits ($513.00) with me to camp. I will invest the money and I *will double it. I knew you would never let me do it if I asked. But you'll be glad I did.*

Your Financial Consultant,
Victoria Chubb

For a second I was too shocked to speak. The nerve of Victoria to think that she could just walk off with our money!

"Are you going to call the police on her?" Tommy asked.

"I don't know," I said. "If we do, it will serve her right."

"Let me know," Tommy said. He reached over and shut out the light as I started back to my room.

"Listen to this!" I cried, charging into my room waving the note. "Can you believe this?" In a voice so angry I hardly recognized it as my own, I read them the note.

"What if she triples our money?" Buck asked.

"She could also lose it all!" Lizzie said sharply. "She has got to be stopped before she ruins us."

"The stock market is like gambling. What does Victoria Chubb know about stocks? She's only twelve years old," Gina said angrily.

"So what are we going to do?" I asked.

"I know," Gina said. "Let's call her Uncle Phil.

Do you still have his card, Roger? We can call him at work. Maybe he'll have an idea."

Luckily, I had put Phil's card on my desk. He wasn't in, but he called us back a few minutes later. He listened as I explained what had happened. For a few seconds he didn't say anything.

Finally he said, "I'm afraid this time Victoria has gone too far. You kids have worked too hard to have her take off with your money. And with her parents away, I can't stand by and do nothing about it." He was silent for a few more seconds. Then he surprised me by saying, "It seems to me the only solution is to find Victoria at camp immediately. We can see how much damage — or good — she's done. Would you care to ride along with me? The camp is about seventy-five miles north. We could be there by dinnertime tonight."

And that's how, an hour later, we found ourselves squeezed into Phil Chubb's little red car, heading up the highway to Victoria's investment camp.

11

Before we left with Phil Chubb the four of us told our folks where we were going. I wrote Mom and Dad a note explaining what had happened. Then I woke up Tommy again. He actually offered to call them at dinnertime from Cindy's to tell them not to worry. It made me a little nervous to see him being so nice. I think he figured our money was already gone, and he felt sorry for me. But I told him to go ahead and do it anyway.

Lizzie got her father on the phone. He'd had a bad day on the golf course and told her he was familiar with the Chubb family, and that with Victoria's note, which he advised us to keep in a safe place, we had a possible case against her. He said he'd be glad to represent us if we decided to go to small claims court. That was pretty good news; but it was a little scary, too. It looked as if we might get our money back after all, but we'd have to go to court to do it.

As he'd promised, Phil pulled up in front of my house a short time later. He honked, and we went running out. Buck landed the front seat, and I squeezed in back with Gina and Lizzie.

"So, how does this investment camp work?" Buck asked as we headed up the four-lane highway toward the Adirondack Mountains, where Victoria's camp was located.

"It's a pretty strict place from what I understand," Phil told us. "They do the usual — swimming, horseback riding, hiking, and crafts. But the campers are also required to spend two hours a day in classroom instruction on the stock market. And each camper has his or her own computer. They learn to feed in any information they think is important from the newspaper or business magazines. They study and analyze the information and then they decide where they want to invest."

"Do you think Victoria's already invested our money?" Gina asked.

"Hard to tell," Phil said. "The camp started on Saturday, so this is her third day. Knowing Victoria, she probably has invested some of it. She'd want to impress the other campers, to show them how smart and good with money she is."

No one said a word, but I couldn't help but think Phil certainly knew his niece very well. She was a total show-off when it came to money.

"You see," Phil continued. "Victoria comes from a family where money is offered instead of love and attention. Take this summer, for instance. Her parents are in Europe for six weeks, and Victoria was home alone with a housekeeper — a very expensive housekeeper, no denying that, but it doesn't matter. Basically, Victoria can buy anything she wants. Unfortunately she can't get the one thing she really wants, a group of friends who truly like her. That's why when you all started up your business she was so envious."

"Is that why she tried to shut us down?" Gina asked.

"I don't think she really meant to do that," Phil said. "She wanted you to see how much she knew about the restaurant business. And that she had connections with influential people. Like me," he said with a smile. "She really only wanted to be part of your group."

For a second we were silent. I was starting to feel a little sorry for Victoria. But I also thought someone should tell her that if she wanted to have friends, she was going about it in all the wrong ways.

"Does this camp have any sessions on making friends?" I asked.

"I don't know," Phil said. "Victoria showed me the information they sent her. They have sessions on current events, finance, and they're big on nutrition. I know they have strict rules about eating healthy foods. No sweets are allowed."

I thought back quickly to Bart in the supermarket. Suddenly it occurred to me that maybe he wasn't buying all that sweet stuff for himself. That would be just like Victoria — to hire him to shop for her. She was probably as tired of grocery shopping as we were.

"The campers can earn badges for athletic teamwork and cooperative spirit, things like that," Phil went on. "I think the whole experience could be good for Victoria. "Which," he said, pausing to look quickly at us, "is why I hope we can get your money back with the least amount of disruption."

"What do you mean?" Lizzie asked.

"I just mean maybe we can find Victoria ourselves, get the money, and no one at camp will have to know. . . ."

"I think they should know she took it without permission," Buck said.

"What's the point?" Phil asked. "Her reputation with you guys at home is shot. Why ruin her reputation away from home, too?"

No one answered, but I thought to myself, Because she deserves it. But since Phil was being so nice to bring us all the way up there, I couldn't say it.

Almost an hour and a half after we left town, Phil turned off the highway. We drove through two small towns which led to a bumpy road that gradually grew steeper. "The turnoff should be somewhere along here," Phil said. The road had tall, thick, sweet-smelling pine forest on either side. There was little traffic, and the woods were still and unmarked except for an occasional sign along the way.

"Look for something that says 'Point of Pine'," Phil instructed us. "That's the name of the camp."

We all watched as various signs flashed by every half mile or so. BIG ED'S VARIETY, 5 MILES AHEAD; THE CABIN — STEAKS, CHOPS, AND SEAFOOD, EARLY BIRD SPECIAL STARTS AT FOUR-THIRTY. Finally we spotted it: POINT OF PINE CAMP — NEXT RIGHT.

Phil turned off the mountain road onto a gravel lane barely wide enough for two cars to pass. "I hope we don't meet a bus coming from the other direction," he joked as we bounced along.

The gravel road led us to a white picket fence that stretched out of sight in two directions. We drove through an open gate and up a short hill to a square white building with green shutters. All along the hillside were a half dozen smaller green-shuttered buildings, and in the distance were a big red barn, a round, lacy-looking gazebo, and a shimmering silver lake. A long dock stretched into the lake, where a row of canoes bobbed on the water.

"This place is great!" Buck said as we stopped before a square building. "Look at that lake. I wonder if they'd let me take a quick canoe ride." But before we could get out of the car, a tall man with thick silver hair, dressed in blue jeans, a blue button-down shirt and a red tie, came striding out of the building.

"May I help you?" he asked politely, but without much friendliness.

"I'm Phil Chubb, Victoria's uncle." Phil hopped out of the car and extended his hand to the man. I hesitantly opened the back door. I didn't know about anyone else, but my legs were stiff from sitting crowded in the back seat for so long.

"I'm Mark Greystone, the director of Point of Pine," the man said. "Is there something wrong?"

"Oh, no," Phil said quickly. "It just happens that Victoria is a friend of these young people." Phil nodded to us as everyone started out of the car. "They've been working together on a summer project," Phil went on. "And it seems when my niece left town she unintentionally took some important documents with her."

Unintentional, my foot! I thought. And since when were ten-, five-, and one-dollar bills documents? But I stood by quietly and let Phil handle everything.

"I was just hoping we might get a chance to speak with her and find out if she has the documents with her, or if she left them somewhere at home," Phil went on smoothly.

"I don't see any harm in that," Mr. Greystone said. "She's in Cabin Seven, I believe. And you young people feel free to look around. We've still got a few openings left."

"How much does it cost to come here for a week?" Buck asked.

Mr. Greystone gave Buck a tolerant but forced smile. He seemed to be looking directly at the hole in Buck's T-shirt, where a small portion of his stomach was poking through. "You just tell your parents you're interested, young man," he said. "They can discuss the finances with me. Now, let me show you to Cabin Seven."

I could pretty much figure out why Mr. Greystone didn't want to talk prices with us. Just from the little I could see of Point of Pine I could tell it would cost a lot to go there. From behind one of the buildings I could smell the delicious aroma of meat cooking on a grill. Off in the distance I saw a long, white fence. Behind it, several horses grazed. Not far from that were four tennis courts and a long chain fence. I figured a pool was probably in back of it.

We followed Mr. Greystone across the grassy lawn of Point of Pine. None of the four of us said a word. I think we were all so amazed to find ourselves here that we couldn't think of a thing to say. We passed the gazebo. A book entitled *A Teenager's Guide to Finance* had been left on the steps. By the lake I saw two campers standing together, looking out at the water. I wondered if they were discussing swimming or investing.

We followed Mr. Greystone down a narrow trail thickly covered with pine needles. It felt like a cushion beneath our feet. The air was cool, and as we walked along in silence, with only the rustle of a small breeze or a small animal or bird moving in the woods around us, I felt I was a million miles away from home, from Aces, and from the Grand Union. Lizzie looked at me and rolled her eyes, and Gina shook her head and gave me a smile. I could see they were as impressed as I was.

"Here we are," Mr. Greystone announced, turning off the trail suddenly. A small white cabin was before us. He knocked on the door, then we entered. What a shock to see a dozen computer terminals lined up along the plain wooden walls of this simple cabin in the woods! This place *did* have everything! Next year, I thought, maybe I would ask my parents if I could come here.

The cabin was as quiet as a library. Three or four campers were hunched over their screens, which displayed lists of words and numbers. They looked up when we entered, then turned their eyes back to the screens. All of them, that is, except one.

A dark, curly head with a pale face had looked up from a terminal in the corner of the cabin. Victoria Chubb jumped up from the swivel chair she had been sitting on. "What are you doing here?" she cried as we approached her.

"We're here — " Gina began.

Phil stopped her. "We just came by to check on some documents regarding the business you people were involved in this summer," he said smoothly. "Do you have them with you?"

I glanced at Mr. Greystone. He wasn't paying too much attention to us anymore. He had been stopped by one of the campers and was now leaning over his shoulder examining his screen with a serious frown. From the stern expression on his face it looked like the stock market was taking a dip that very instant.

"What documents?" Victoria asked.

"You know what documents," Lizzie hissed. "The *green* documents."

"I left you a note," Victoria said. But as she said it I saw a look of fear and shame cross her face. A bright flush crept into her snowy pale cheeks, and she began to squint. With a half fist she wiped her hand across her face. Victoria Chubb was going to cry.

"Have you invested the money yet?" Phil asked her in a low voice.

Victoria nodded. She sniffed. "In Mid-Day," she whimpered.

"Mid-Day?" Phil asked. "What's that?"

"It's a company," Victoria said in a shaky voice. "A brand-new company." She looked at us. "Mid-Day," she repeated. "I first got interested in it because that's when Aces is open. Get it? At mid-day." Buck rolled his eyes and Lizzie shook her head. It didn't sound like a very intelligent way to pick a stock.

"So I did some research." Victoria gave a loud sniff. She looked away from us, then went on in a tiny voice. "The stock is new, so it was cheap."

"What does Mid-Day do?" Gina asked.

"They make a new kind of light bulb," Victoria said. "Suppose you turn on a light at six o'clock at night. If it's still sunny outside it just shines a little. At seven it gets brighter, at eight brighter still, and by nine o'clock when it's dark outside, the light bulb is on all the way. It saves on electricity. And the bulbs last longer. And they say you don't get the shock of sudden bright light. The people at Mid-Day say it's better for your eyes."

"They would," Lizzie muttered.

I blurted out, "You invested our five hundred dollars in light bulbs!"

"Just a second," Phil interrupted. "What about your own money, the money your parents gave you to invest?"

"I spent a little of it," Victoria admitted.

"On sweets?" I asked.

"Yes," Victoria said, looking away. "But I've been sharing them with the other campers. They're my friends now. No one else thought to bring up any candy or cookies for the week."

Just like Victoria, I thought. Trying to buy herself friends with bribes of caramel crunch cookies and candy bars.

"How much was a little?" Phil asked.

"About sixty dollars," Victoria said. "I bought some clothes, too. You see, that's why I needed your money. Because with a lot of companies there's a minimum you have to invest. I didn't know that. If I didn't have enough money I couldn't buy a lot of stocks."

"So how much Mid-Day do we own?" Lizzie asked her.

"One hundred three shares," Victoria said. "When I bought it, it was five dollars a share. I took five hundred and thirteen dollars from Aces. I put in the extra two dollars to make it even."

"Big of you," Lizzie said sarcastically. "What's it worth now?"

Victoria turned to her computer. She pressed a few keys. She watched the screen intently. We all leaned over her shoulder. A long list of names began to pass down the screen. Suddenly Victoria stopped the moving list, and sure enough the word *Mid-Day* appeared on the left-hand side. A bunch of numbers flashed on across from it. Victoria frowned. "It's down," she said with a frown. "Four ninety-six a share."

"So we've lost money," Gina said flatly.

"But it may go up again," Victoria said.

"And it may go down further," I pointed out. But a strange thing was happening. I was getting the same excited, grown-up feeling just talking about owning stock that I had gotten when we had first started planning our business.

Phil glanced at his watch. "We've got to get

going," he said. "I suggest you four discuss this together outside for a few minutes. Decide what you want Victoria to do. She can sell Mid-Day the first thing tomorrow and give back the money at a loss — which she'll make up. Or you can keep it in the market for a while, until the end of the week at least, when she leaves camp. Maybe Mid-Day will go up again. And then you'd get back more money than you invested."

The four of us filed outside. We stood in a circle under a tall pine tree and discussed it. "Actually, the idea for those light bulbs isn't bad," Lizzie said. "They could catch on. We could make a lot of money."

"But the stock is down," Gina pointed out, running some purple gloss along her lips. "Why? Maybe the light bulbs don't work. We have to consider that."

"Give them time to catch on," Buck said. "I think we should keep the money in Mid-Day until *we* decide to pull it out. Victoria can be our broker."

"I like that," I said. "We don't really need the money this week. We can buy supplies out of what we make. And if these bulbs catch on, we could do very well."

Finally we voted, and it was four to zero to take a chance and let Victoria keep our money in Mid-

Day, at least until the end of her stay at camp. The only directions we gave her were if the stock went down to four dollars, she was to sell — we'd bail out then. To protect ourselves we put the whole agreement in writing. Phil was our witness, and we all signed it.

"I'll call you the second I get home," Victoria said as she walked us to the car.

"You'd better," I grumbled. I still couldn't forgive her for all the trouble she'd put us through.

"Look," she said. "I'm sorry I took the money without asking. I didn't ever mean to steal from you. I just wanted . . ." Victoria couldn't go on. Her face had turned all red again and her eyes had gotten that squinty look.

I turned away. I didn't want to watch her cry, and I figured I knew what she was trying to say she wanted. She wanted us to like her. And that made me feel bad. Because even though she tried she always seemed to be trying the wrong way. Suddenly I didn't care about the money, Mid-Day stock, or even being mad at Victoria. I just wanted to go home.

"We'll talk to you when you get back," I mumbled, climbing into the back seat. Gina and Buck followed me, with Lizzie getting in the front for the ride back. Phil gave Victoria a big hug and a kiss before we drove off.

On the way home we stopped, and Phil treated us to hamburgers, fries, and milk shakes. "You all handled that situation very well," he told us. "You had the right to be a lot madder than you acted. I hope Victoria appreciates it. And learns her lesson."

"Thanks, Phil," Gina said, stifling a yawn as she finished the rest of her shake. She was sound asleep in the car soon after our quick stop for dinner, and she didn't wake up until Phil dropped her off at her house. Buck, Lizzie, and I weren't talking too much, either. I knew we were all tired, and I was wondering if Phil was right — if Victoria would learn her lesson.

I hoped so, too. But I doubted it. I wasn't sure people like Victoria Chubb could ever really change. But I had another thought. I realized it when my parents came rushing out to meet me as I got out of Phil's car around nine o'clock that night. They wanted to hear everything, and they kept glancing at me and at each other, looking very impressed as I told them the story. The thought that occurred to me was that *this* was something Victoria Chubb apparently didn't have — a family that cared about her.

"Hey, Dad," I said, after I had told them all about the camp, the horses, the lake, and the computer cabin. "Next summer that might be a good place for me. I bet it wouldn't cost that much."

My father put his arm around my shoulder. "You know, Roger," he said. "I really like the way you're making money on your own now. And I bet you've learned as much running the luncheonette as you would at any camp. But we'll see. Next summer's still quite a ways off."

Suddenly very tired, I headed to my room. My bed looked especially good to me, and later, I realized we hadn't seen the sleeping cabins at Point of Pines. But no bunk, no matter how fancy the camp, could ever be as comfortable as my own bed felt that very moment.

12

For the rest of the week we followed Mid-Day stock in the newspaper. My father showed us how to read the stock market columns, and he even called that Thursday to tell me it had gone up again. "Four-ninety-eight!" he exclaimed, sounding more excited than I was. "You may top five before the week's over."

The next week we held our last business meeting. It was the Friday before Labor Day, and we had two big decisions to make. First, what should we do about the money? In order to keep it invested, all four partners had to agree. And second, we had to plan our Grand Closing.

We decided to spend the first few minutes planning the closing, then invite Victoria in for our decision about Mid-Day.

Planning the Grand Closing was pretty simple. We all agreed it should be business-as-usual, with a few extras thrown in. We decided to decorate the garage and offer something free to eat with each meal. We figured watermelon would be a good, inexpensive, and popular choice.

"Isn't Victoria supposed to be at this meeting?" Buck asked, dropping a banana peel into my wastebasket.

"I told her to be here at one-thirty," I said. It was a quarter of two and there was still no sign of her. "I told her we'd want the latest figures on what Mid-Day is worth. We have to decide whether to hold on to it or sell."

"I say sell," Gina said. "It was four-ninety-nine yesterday. So what if we lose a few pennies?"

"I agree," Buck said. "I want that twelve-speed before it snows. Let's take the money and run."

"I'd like to hold on to it," I said. It wasn't greed; it was just that with Aces closed for the season I was already beginning to miss that excited feeling I got from doing something grown-up. Keeping money in the stock market was a good way to continue feeling that way. "What about you, Lizzie?"

"I don't know," Lizzie said with a frown. "I could use the money. But right now we've lost money. If we wait we might gain some."

"But we haven't lost much," Gina argued.

"Yes, but — " I began. The ringing of the doorbell interrupted me. "That's probably Victoria," I said.

It was, and she followed me upstairs. I noticed her pale skin looked a little tan, and something about her seemed quieter. "So, what's going on? You're not going to sell now, are you?" she asked.

"We haven't voted yet," I said. I could tell Victoria wanted us to hold on, and even though I wouldn't usually take sides with her, for once I liked her thinking. "At camp they told us that stocks take time to grow," she said, "like plants."

And like some people, I wanted to add. But I said, "Why don't you tell that to the others? I think some of them want to sell now."

Victoria did. She sat on the edge of my bed and tried to explain to Buck, Gina, and Lizzie that we have to give Mid-Day a chance. "It's not the same as the luncheonette," she said. "With that you could start seeing profits almost immediately. With a stock it's different. Yesterday Mid-Day was at four-ninety-nine. Today it's four-ninety-seven."

"And tomorrow it could be at two-twenty-nine," Gina interrupted. "We could lose everything overnight."

"And we could triple our money, too," I said,

sounding more like Victoria than I ever thought I would.

"We should vote," Lizzie said. "I'm voting with Roger. I don't think we'll lose that much. And I don't really need the money right now."

"I'm voting with Gina," Buck said. "I need the money."

There was a moment of silence. We'd never, in all the decisions we'd had to make, had a tie. To my surprise I found myself looking to Victoria.

"As your business consultant, I can tell you some things you can do," Victoria said. "You could take out Gina and Buck's money now and keep Roger's and Lizzie's in."

I made a face. "We're all in this together," I said. "It's really Aces money."

"Yeah," Buck said. "We're partners. One goes out, we all go out."

Lizzie and Gina nodded, so Victoria went on. "You could set a date that everyone agrees on. And on that day, you sell. No matter what."

We silently considered that for a second. "Or," Victoria went on. "You could make me the fifth partner. I could vote and break the tie."

"What about setting a date?" Gina said quickly. "When I think of it, I want the money for school clothes. The first few weeks I'll still be wearing summer stuff. I can hold off a little while."

"October first?" Buck asked. "That might be a good date to sell — unless it hits four before that. Then we bail out immediately."

"October first sounds good to me," I said.

"Me, too," Lizzie said.

"I'll go along with that," Gina agreed.

"Wise decision," Victoria said, standing up. For a second I thought she might be mad because her attempt to become a partner didn't go over too well. But she just seemed pleased we'd come to a decision. "I have to get going," she said, starting for the door.

"By the way, we're having our Grand Closing on Labor Day," I told her before she left. "That's the day the pool closes. It'll be the last day for deliveries, too. We're inviting some people who helped with the luncheonette, and so we'd like to have your Uncle Phil stop over, too."

"And, Victoria, do you know Bart's phone number?" Lizzie asked.

"I've got it in my files at home," Victoria said. "I'll call you and give it to you tonight." She gave us a big smile before she left, and as her curly head disappeared behind my bedroom door I had the strange thought that maybe, like Mid-Day, Victoria Chubb, too, just needed time to grow. Or maybe I did. Ordinarily that remark about her files at home would have really annoyed me. For some reason today it didn't bother me at all.

For the Grand Closing we decided to go all out. We spent ten dollars on streamers, balloons, and poster boards. We made up six farewell signs that said: THANK YOU FOR YOUR BUSINESS — SEE YOU NEXT YEAR! and hung them around my garage and yard. We made six more announcing the Grand Closing and posted them around the neighborhood. A FREE SLICE OF WATERMELON WITH EVERY LUNCH! we wrote on them.

"I was just reading this article about first impressions," Lizzie told us as we stood waiting for our customers to arrive that Labor Day. Everything was ready. My dad, who didn't have to go to work that day, had offered to slice the watermelons, and my mom had donated heavy plastic plates to serve them on. "First impressions count a lot," Lizzie was saying. "But last impressions can be just as important. I think having a Grand Closing is leaving a good last impression on our customers."

"I agree," I said, looking around the garage. It looked great. Red, white, and blue streamers hung from the four corners. We'd joined them together in the center and hung a bunch of red balloons from them. I had on my best jeans and a shirt I hadn't worn since school let out. Buck had actually gotten a haircut. His dad had insisted on it before school began, telling him he wouldn't be able to see the blackboard if he didn't. Lizzie had on an orange shirt that matched her orange shorts. But Gina looked the most festive. She had on a white T-shirt covered with sparkling sequins, silky-looking white pants, and long, glittery earrings.

"This isn't a prom," Buck grumbled at her, looking at her fingernails, which she'd covered with a white, sparking polish. "We still have to work you know, Gina."

"I know," Gina said. "But a Grand Closing should be a special occasion. That way people won't forget us next year. Don't worry, I'll work." And it was true — no matter how dressed up she was, Gina always worked as hard as anyone else.

It was eleven twenty-five. There was a knock on the garage door. "Let's open," I said. We'd already sent Bart and Victoria off with a dozen lunches for the pool. Now it was time to serve the neighborhood customers.

We pulled up the door. The Waters crew stood waiting. "Thought we'd get here early before you ran out of that free watermelon," Mr. Waters told us, leading his three boys up to the table.

I called into the kitchen. "Dad! Customers are

here!" My father came hurrying out. We'd sat up a special table for him. Two huge watermelons were on it. He took a big knife and cut one in half.

"Wow," said the littlest Waters' boy eyeing the balloons and streamers. "This is just like a party."

And pretty soon it *was* a party. Dao and Kathy showed up with not only their little charges, but also their two boyfriends. "What if one of us finds a marked bag today?" Dao asked.

"You'll get a certificate for the Grand Opening next year," Lizzie told her.

"We'll be here," Dao said.

Mrs. Lingreen came up the walk and stood for a while talking to my mother. I saw her nodding approvingly at us and my mother smiling proudly. I felt proud, too. Proud that I'd been able to prove to my mother that I could keep out of trouble — without checking in with anyone. Mrs. Lingreen ordered her usual half sandwich, said she'd love a small slice of watermelon, and then added in her gentle voice that she was going to try one of Lizzie's M&M cookies instead of an apple today. "I suppose at the Grand Closing I can go off my diet," she said, giving me a quick, soft smile.

After that it seemed everyone came at once. Kids we'd been serving all summer and kids we'd never seen before suddenly started piling into the garage. Gina's parents and little Lester Winchell

II made a noisy arrival the same time Buck's folks did. The Buckleys seemed to have given up their diets for the day, too, because they ordered the full lunch and then got in line for watermelon. Lizzie's mom came, (her father was golfing), and Tommy made a special effort to get up early.

He was leaving for college the following day, so he invited Cindy over to join him for lunch. For a second, between customers, I watched them eating. Tommy's mustache had become a thick, dark line above his lips. I'd have to tell him how neat it looked before he left, I thought, suddenly realizing how much I was going to miss him. Even though I hadn't seen him much this summer, the idea that he wouldn't be living here anymore was going to be hard to get used to.

It was well after one o'clock when the last customer was served and my father laid down his watermelon knife. "Can the hired help eat now?" he called. "My mouth has been watering for one of those sandwiches since noon."

"Sure, Dad, go ahead," I told him. "What would you like?" It sounded funny, me being the boss, while my dad asked permission to eat.

"I'll have a tuna spade and a carton of milk. How about you, Joan?" he called to my mother. She was sitting with Lizzie's mom.

"I'll have a good old peanut-butter-and-jelly heart with a grape juice," my mother answered. "And Lizzie, you've got to share your recipe with me. Those cookies look wonderful."

I was just cutting out my mother's peanut-butter-and-jelly heart when Phil Chubb's small red car pulled up. "We'll need two more pieces of watermelon, please, Dad," I told my father. "Better make that three," I added. Bart had climbed out of the back of Phil's car, too.

"A Grand Closing, what a clever idea," Phil said as he, Victoria, and Bart stood ready to order. "I've been to a lot of Grand Openings, but never to a Grand Closing."

"We're glad you could come," Lizzie told him. "If it weren't for you, we might have had just a plain closing. About two months ago." She gave Victoria a wary look and then asked them all what they wanted.

"Have you heard anything about Mid-Day?" I asked Victoria. Bart gave her a knowing look.

"Has she ever," he said, actually sounding pretty excited.

"What?" I demanded.

Victoria grinned and Phil looked pleased, too. "Tell them," he urged her.

"Well, I was talking to my father today, and he

just read in one of his business magazines that three big cities in Alaska have ordered thousands of Mid-Day light bulbs to test during the dark season up there. According to him, the stock should go way over five when the market opens on Tuesday."

"Super!" Buck cried. "I say we sell on Tuesday."

"What about October first?" Lizzie asked him. "If it's over five on Tuesday, in another month it could be over six. Or even seven."

"It is my professional opinion that you should hold on to it as long as you can," Victoria said, in the superior tone I had hoped she was getting over.

Gina was nodding her head in agreement. "The October first deadline still holds," she said.

"Right," I added. "I don't think we should even discuss it until then."

"Fine," Buck said. "Then let's discuss next summer's business plans. I have a few ideas for changes around here." He thoughtfully surveyed the garage for a moment.

Victoria took advantage of his silence. "I want you all to be the first to know that next summer I'm offering a course on investments at my house," she announced importantly. "I'll be the instructor. After all, I've graduated from investment camp. I can teach you all I know. And I'll be charging a lot less than Point of Pine charges. Plus, my students can use my pool."

Lizzie rolled her eyes, and I looked down at the slice of watermelon on my lap. Victoria Chubb would never stop surprising me. Did she really think anyone would want to become one of *her* students?

"So, what changes do you think we should make, Buck?" Gina asked. I guess she wasn't too eager to sign up for Victoria's class, either.

"We've got to grow," Buck said slowly. "I see — customers sitting at tables next year and maybe — "

Victoria interrupted. "Just because I'll be teaching my course doesn't mean I won't be around to consult. My records on Aces show that until Bart and I started the delivery business you weren't making much of a profit."

"We were doing okay," I said sharply.

"Okay isn't good enough in business," Victoria retorted. "Next year you'll need a full-time consultant. Especially if you plan to have Aces grow."

"I was thinking we could put in tables next year," Buck said. "And maybe a salad bar."

"I've got a few others ideas, too," Victoria said.

"Me, too," I said. However, I didn't go on. How could I say that my ideas had to do with Victoria Chubb? Like maybe she could take lessons on being a nice person? Or maybe she could go to a special school where they trained you to get along with other people?

Because Victoria still didn't seem to realize what a know-it-all she was. "I could either consult full-time or become a partner," she was saying. "But you have to let me know soon. I have other offers."

No one answered that. But Buck smiled as he went on. "What about serving hot dogs, hamburgers, and possibly even steak?" he asked. "And for dessert, if Mid-Day light bulbs pay off, we could have Baked Alaska!"

At the mention of Baked Alaska, Lizzie spit the first watermelon seed at him. I followed, and pretty soon Bart, Victoria, and Gina were all clobbering him with little black seeds. Across the yard I could see my mother smiling, and as I gave her a wave I figured I was finally beginning to understand how adults thought. At least I understood what she meant when she said you never knew what a good time you could have working. And you learned a lot, too. You learned about jobs, but you also learned about people. People like Buck, Gina, and Lizzie. But especially about people like Victoria Chubb.

About the Author

JOYCE HUNT is the author of several short stories and articles that have been published in *Highlights*, *Cobblestone*, and *Child Life*. This is her first novel. An elementary school teacher, she wrote *Eat Your Heart Out, Victoria Chubb* because she feels it is important for kids to learn how to get along with different kinds of people, including the Victoria Chubbs. Ms. Hunt enjoys running, biking, and cross-country skiing, and lives in Delmar, New York, with her cat, Cantaloupe.